Octavia Barry

The Lady Victoria Tylney Long Wellesley

A Memoir

Octavia Barry

The Lady Victoria Tylney Long Wellesley
A Memoir

ISBN/EAN: 9783337112042

Printed in Europe, USA, Canada, Australia, Japan

Cover: Foto ©Raphael Reischuk / pixelio.de

More available books at **www.hansebooks.com**

The Lady Victoria Tylney Long Wellesley.

A MEMOIR.

BY

HER ELDEST GOD-DAUGHTER.

WITH PORTRAITS AND ILLUSTRATIONS.

LONDON:

SKEFFINGTON & SON, PICCADILLY,

PUBLISHERS TO H.M. THE QUEEN AND H.R.H. THE PRINCE OF WALES.

1899.

Preface.

For the materials of this Memoir I am much indebted
to Captain Long, who placed before me the large correspondence bequeathed to him by the late Lady Victoria
Wellesley, and also supplied me with most of the illustrations. The Vicar of All Souls', Eastbourne, kindly
supervised my account of the Church. I also owe many
thanks to a kind friend who lent me several curious books,
referring to the history of the Longs of Wiltshire. The
frontispiece is from a copper-plate engraving of a miniature
taken by Miss Scott, of Lady Victoria Wellesley when
she was about seven years old. The plate is by
Gimber. The other illustrations possess a certain
value of their own from the associations which sur-
round them.

South Wraxall may be considered the cradle of the
Long family. Draycot Cerne was also their ancient
manor. Its Park was considered by Aubrey the finest
in Wiltshire.

The prints of Wanstead House are valuable on account
of their representing a place which can be seen no more.

Of the once magnificent mansion, which excelled even Blenheim in its splendour, nothing now remains but the waste ground on which it stood, opposite Wanstead lake, in Essex. The pictures of this place are in private possession, and the engraver has done his best to smooth out the creases of age which may yet be seen in the illustration.

The impression of Unsted Wood is taken from a pencil sketch of David Cox, made during one of his visits to the house. The portraits of Lady Victoria Wellesley and her brother are faithful likenesses. West Stoke House will, I hope, convey to many friends the remembrance of the hospitalities which Lady Victoria delighted in dispensing. All Souls' Church, Eastbourne, has only one other Church like it in the Kingdom, and that is at Wilton, near Salisbury. Draycot Church contains, within its chancel, some curious brasses of Sir Edward and Lady Cerne, once the possessors of Draycot. In a vault in the Church, now sealed up, probably for ever, repose the remains of many generations of the Tylney Longs, of whom Lady Victoria Long Wellesley was the last representative. The illustrations of Draycot Church and the Keeper's Lodge, in Draycot Park, are from pencil sketches taken by my sister, Miss Barry.

Contents.

List of Illustrations.

x.

Introduction.

My Godmother! A host of recollections crowd into my mind at the mention of that name. In recalling the past I seem to picture her as she used to look, dressed for a party in all the grandeur of velvet, lace and jewellery. Imagination recalls her entering my bedchamber—unexpected, yet ever welcome. I seem to see her, as of old, in the cottages of the poor, fondling their babies and giving them kind and cheering words; or visiting with equal grace in the mansions of the rich, carrying with her the charm of her fascinating manners. Again she is beside me in Church, with her reverent demeanour, as she used to kneel, wrapped in devotion, before the Throne of Grace. I seem, in imagination, to walk with her again by the health-giving waves of Eastbourne, or in her gardens and shrubberies at Bolney and at West Stoke. She comes back to me as she looked when I sat beside her in her beautiful carriage, taking long and happy drives far off into the country. Memory recalls her sympathizing ways, her affection and her faithful love. Again her wise words and good advice seem to sound in my ears, and what from her was, as Tennyson describes, " soft rebukes in blessings ended." Again she enfolds me in her warm embrace, and gives me her tender kisses. The past is fast placing these pleasant recollections in the distance, but still they are near to me. Her portrait is before me in the room, which is full of the mementoes of her affection. Therefore it is no wonder that, in reverence and love, my thoughts so often turn to one who was a very central figure in my life, and who exercised on me, as she did on all around her, a happy and beneficial influence.

The Lady Victoria Tylney Long Wellesley.

CHAPTER I.

The Longs of Bygone Time.

LADY Victoria Catherine Mary Pole Tylney Long Wellesley was the daughter of the fourth, and the only sister of the fifth, Earl of Mornington. Her great grandfather,[1] Garrett Colley Wellesley, who was the first Earl of Mornington,[2] had five sons. The eldest was created Marquis Wellesley, and succeeded his father as second Earl of Mornington; the second son was created Baron Maryborough; the third was Arthur, first Duke of Wellington; the fourth,

[1] Through the marriage of Garrett Wellesley's grandfather, Henry Colley, with Mary Usher, the Wellesley's were also connected with the family of Archbishop Usher.

[2] He composed the " Mornington Chant," which is found in most Hymn Books.

A

Gerald Valonian, Canon of St. Paul's; the fifth, Henry, created Lord Cowley, whose two sons were afterwards Lord Cowley, Ambassador at Paris, and the Honourable Gerald Wellesley, Dean of Windsor. As the Marquis of Wellesley died without children, the Earldom of Mornington devolved on his next brother, Baron Maryborough. His son became, in due course, the fourth Earl of Mornington. Therefore his two sons, William Arthur, the fifth Earl, the Honourable James Fitzroy, and his only daughter, Lady Victoria Catherine Mary, were the grandchildren of Lord Maryborough, and, consequently, the great-nephews and niece of the famous Duke of Wellington. It will also be perceived that Lady Victoria's father was first cousin to Lord Cowley, Ambassador at Paris, and to the Honourable Gerald Wellesley, Dean of Windsor.

The name of Pole was assumed by Lady Victoria's great-grandfather, the first Earl, upon his inheriting the estates of his cousin, Mr. William Pole, of Ballyfin, Ireland. Lord Maryborough's three daughters (who were, of course, Lady Victoria's aunts) were married, the eldest, Mary, to a son of Lord Bagot; the second, Priscilla, to Lord Burghersh, eldest son of the Earl of Westmoreland ; the third, Emily, to the youngest son of the Duke of Beaufort.

From her mother (who was the richest heiress in the kingdom), Lady Victoria bore the name of Tylney

Long, and through her she was descended from one of the oldest families in England. For the ancient family of Long dates back to the reign of Ethelred, when they were tenants of the Manor of Bradford under the Abbess of Shaftesbury. Here they continued until the Dissolution, when they were able to purchase their rights. Leland, who wrote in 1550, says: " Mr. Long hath a little Manor about a mile from Monkton Farley, at Wrexley." He also gives this quaint account of the origin of the name of Long : " One Long Thomas, a stoute felow, was sette up by one of the old Lordes Hungerford, and after, because this Thomas was called Long Thomas, Long after was usurped for the name of the family. This Master Long Thomas had some lands by Hungerforde's procuration." Camden, who wrote in 1586, gives a somewhat similar account. He states it thus: " A young gentleman of the name of Preux, being of tall stature, attending on the Lord Hungerford, was among his fellows called Long H., who after, preferred to a good marriage by his lord, was called H. Long. That name continued to his posterity, knights and men of great worship." However, these stories, if they can be received, must belong to a much earlier date ; also the tradition of the connection of the Longs with the family of Preux may have been caused by the ancient motto of the Long's *Pieux quoique Preux.*

If great height gave rise to the name of Long, it is a curious fact that, in later times, the Longs should all have been small men. The ancestor, to whom the pedigree can be most clearly traced back, was Robert Long, Knight of the Shire of Wilts in 1433. He was a feoffee and confidential friend of Walter, Lord Hungerford, the Lord High Treasurer, and he also associated with Sir Humphrey Stafford and other men of note.

Canon Jackson states that, through Robert Long's mother, who was a Berkeley, the estate of Wraxall passed into the Long family. It was also in Robert Long's time that the beautiful estate of Draycot Cerne, in Wilts, became their property. This place, since the reign of Richard the Second, had passed through the hands of the St. Germains, the Venoirs, and the Cernes. Aubrey relates that the last of the Cernes, having died without children in 1430, the Draycot estates were to pass to a distant cousin, John Herynge, after the death of Richard Cerne's mother, who had possession of the estate for her life. John Herynge, however, sold his reversionary interest to Robert Long, of Wraxall, who purchased it for his second son, John. However, in the copy of a letter written in 1688 by James Long, of Draycot (the grandson of Sir Walter Long, of Wraxall and Draycot), it is stated that the daughter and heiress of the last of the Cernes, who was Lord of the

SOUTH WRAXALL MANOR, WILTS.

Manor of Draycot, married a Knight of the name of Weight. Their daughter and heiress, Margaret Weight, married John Long. Draycot, which to this day is called Draycot Cerne, thus passed, by marriage, from the Cernes to the Weights, and from the Weights to the Longs. John Long died before his father, and his son, Sir Thomas Long, inherited Draycot, through his mother, Margaret Weight, the heiress of the Cernes. Sir Robert's eldest son, Henry, was, of course, the heir of Wraxall.

The ancient mansion of Draycot, which was the beloved home of the Longs for at least four hundred years, is situated a few miles to the north-east of Chippenham. The Manor-house of Draycot is a large irregular building, with a park of considerable extent and pleasure-grounds attached to it. The house contains many objects of interest in paintings and Sevres china. The park crowns a hill, commanding an extensive prospect, and is esteemed one of the most beautiful in Wiltshire, being richly studded with magnificent oaks and venerable hawthorns, and abounding with deer. In the pleasure-grounds there are many fine specimens of American plants of all kinds, for which the soil of Draycot is specially congenial.

Thomas, the son of John Long, was one of the company of noblemen who went to meet Henry the Seventh at Taunton, in pursuit of Perkin Warbeck.

He was knighted at the marriage of Prince Arthur, for having greatly distinguished himself at the battle of Theroueme. Henry the Eighth granted him afterwards a new crest, a lion's head erased, crowned with a man's hand in the mouth. Henry Long died in 1490 leaving no children, so his nephew, Thomas Long, of Draycot, inherited Wraxall. Thus the two estates were united, and so they continued until the death of Sir Walter Long in 1610. From John Long, Draycot descended, through eleven generations in male line, to Sir James Tylney Long, the last Baronet.

After the union of the two estates under Thomas Long, they passed to his son, Sir Henry, Sheriff of Wiltshire and Knight of the Shire in 1552.

He was succeeded in 1556 by his son Sir Robert. Then came Sir Robert's son, Sir Walter, who was M.P., in 1592. This Sir Walter Long was a very great man in Wiltshire. Aubrey relates that he kept a trumpeter, and that, when he attended the Sessions at Marlborough, he rode there with thirty servants and retainers, as was the custom for men of his rank in those days.

A peculiar kind of stone having been found at Draycot, with streaks of blue silver ore, which was apt to tinge the water in the wells, Sir Walter had pits sunk at Draycot for the discovery of silver, which, however, ended in very little.

In his time Draycot and Wraxall became separate property, and from very unhappy causes. Sir Walter Long, having first married Mary Packington, had one son, John, who, of course, was his rightful heir. He married, secondly, Catherine, daughter of Sir John Thynne, of Longleat. By her he had another son, called Walter. The second Lady Long, aided by her brother, Sir Egremont Thynne, set to work to prejudice her husband against her stepson, and, at last, succeeded in doing so. The following account of this sad occurrence is abridged from Burke's " Anecdotes of the Aristocracy " :—

" Six weeks after their marriage the happy couple came to the Halls of Draycot. The day of their arrival there was a great occasion for the villagers. Revelry, after the approved old English fashion, prevailed, and all were happy, save one. This sole exceptional person was no other than John, the heir of the houses of Wraxall and Draycot, son of the man who was that day a happy bridegroom, if of somewhat mature years, and of that lady now in her grave, whose place a girl and a stranger had come to fill. John Long, though himself of that disposition which joins in festivities with even reckless enthusiasm, was silent, sad and solitary on the morning of the 'Welcome Home' of his father and his stepmother. John Long was simple and candid in disposition, while at the same time, his affections were warm

and generous.   He never suspected man or woman.
He never took the trouble to consider the motives of
others, or to estimate the weight that interest might
represent in an action apparently spontaneous and
cordial.   Lady Long and her brother Sir Egremont
had thought it worth while to study the character of
the simple and confiding young Master of Draycot
with some attention.   They had hardly been upon
the scene at Draycot for more than a few days when,
from servants and others, they were informed that
the young Master was rather too fond of the wine
bottle and the dice-box.   This knowledge ascer-
tained, their course of conduct was already arrived
at.   Young Long, the heir of all his father's property,
the obstruction in the way of whatever children
might come by the second marriage, must be ruined,
or at least so disgraced as to provoke his father to
disinherit him.   The means of arriving at this end
readily presented themselves.   John's father, Sir
Walter, a man of grave and unrelenting character,
who had already had occasion to visit his son's
peccadilloes heavily upon his head, was, neither
from principle nor from interest, at all given to
lavish pocket money upon the young heir.   His
parsimony was the opportunity for his son's enemies.
They stuffed young Long's pockets with gold, en-
couraged him to take life easily and freely, merely
smiled when, in his presence, they heard of his

excesses, but took good care that all these excesses were magnified into heinous crimes by themselves, and so brought under the notice of the lad's father. Sir Walter, influenced on the one hand by the wiles of his charming wife, on the other by the deeper wiles of his brother-in-law, agreed to make a will, disinheriting his son John, and settling all his property on his second wife and her relations."

Meantime Sir Walter Long had declined in health; was, in fact, on the brink of death. He had now been alienated from his son for a considerable time. He deemed it a sin to make any provision for one who would spend all his possessions in drinking and gambling. Sir Walter, being thus prejudiced against his eldest son, Lady Long never left off her attempts until she induced her husband to disinherit him.

She laid the scene for doing this at Bath, while her brother, Sir Egremont Thynne, an eminent serjeant-at-law, was attending the Assizes. He drew up a draft will and laid it before Sir Walter, who approved of and ordered it to be copied. Sir Egremont's clerk was to sit up all night to engross it. As he was writing, he perceived a shadow on the parchment; he looked up, and there appeared a hand, a lady's delicate white hand, so placed between the light and the deed as to obscure the spot upon which he was engaged. The unaccountable hand,

however, vanished almost as soon as it was noticed.
He was startled at it, but thought it might only be
his fancy, so he wrote on. He had now come to
the worst clause in the whole deed, the clause which
disinherited poor John Long, and which was rendered yet more atrocious by the slanders which it
pleaded in its own justification, and was rapidly
travelling over this black indictment, when for the
second and, after a short interval, for the third time,
the same visionary white hand (he could discern it
was a woman's hand) was thrust forth between the
light and the parchment.

Uttering a yell of horror, the clerk rushed from
the room, woke up Sir Egremont from his midnight
slumbers, and told him his story, adding his belief
that the spectre hand was that of the late Lady
Long. He absolutely refused to go on with the
deed, but it was engrossed by another clerk and duly
signed and sealed. The eldest son was, with all due
form, disinherited, and Sir Walter, dying soon afterwards, left his estates and his great fortune to his
younger son, Walter. Yet the appearance of the
white hand was not without its results. The clerk's
ghastly tale soon got abroad, and his story becoming
a matter of universal conversation, a number of
friends rose up to aid the disinherited heir, who
might otherwise have forgotten him. The body of
the old knight did not go quiet to the grave. It

was arrested at the Church porch by the trustees of the late Lady Long; her nearest relations commenced a suit against the intended heir; and the result was a compromise between the parties. John Long[1] took possession of the smaller property of Wraxall, while his half-brother, Walter, was allowed to retain Draycot. Hence the division of the two estates. I have detailed this Legend of the White Hand at length because, besides its being one of the most curious stories in the annals of the landed gentry, it made a very deep impression upon Lady Victoria Long Wellesley. When the Draycot estates passed away from herself, she was wont to say that the "sins of the fathers were visited upon the children," and that she sometimes thought that the white hand, which sought to arrest Sir Walter Long's unjust deed, was the foreshadowing of her own.

Another sad and very tragical event occurred about this time. This was the murder of Sir Walter Long's younger brother Henry. It is related in the *Wilts Archæological Magazine* that Henry Long, having had a quarrel with Sir Henry and Sir Charles Danvers, one of them shot him openly with a pistol in the inn at Corsham, and that several other county gentlemen were present. Aubrey,

[1] From whom the Right Honourable Walter Long, Minister of Agriculture, is directly descended.

however, states that Henry Long was assassinated in the parlour of the Rectory of Broad Somerford, a village not far from Draycot.

Sir Walter Long died in 1610, the Draycot estates passing, as mentioned before, to his younger son Walter.

CHAPTER II.

―――

Golden Days and Great Possessions.

―――

IN the reign of Charles the Second four hundred and twenty-six Baronets were created. One of these was Colonel James Long, son of Walter Long, of Draycot, and grandson of Sir Walter Long, of Wraxall and Draycot. So he was the first Baronet of the name of Long. Aubrey relates that he was educated at Magdalen College, Oxford, and that he served and distinguished himself in the Civil Wars. In acknowledgment of these services, Charles the Second presented him with a candelabra and a pair of valuable silver dogs, which were in one of the grates at Draycot House, in the time of the last Earl of Mornington, and may be there now.

Sir James Long's favourite sports were horsemanship and falconing. There is a curious advertisement in *The London Gazette* of March 15th, 1676 :—

" Lost, near Malmesbury, in Wiltshire, the 26th

day of February last, an old Tyes Lanner [1] with two vervels, [2] inscribed both Sir James Long's Baronet. Whoever gives notice of him to Mr. Adam Jessope, near St. Clement's Church, Faulconer, or to Sir James Long at Draycutt, near Malmesbury, shall be very well rewarded."

Sir James Long was a great friend of Aubrey, to whom Draycot House was a home in his misfortunes. Aubrey speaks of him in these quaint terms: " He was an admirable orator, a great historian and romancer, and exceedingly curious and searching in natural things." Aubrey makes several allusions to Sir James in his "Natural History of Wiltshire." This historian was also assisted by him in the chapter on " Beasts, Reptiles and Insects." In the original MS. Sir James Long's letters are inserted. Aubrey speaks of Sir James Long as his honoured and faithful friend. He used to meet him at Avebury and accompany him on his hawking expeditions in that neighbourhood. He remarks: " The flight of the falcons was but a parenthesis to the Colonel's facetious discourses, and the Muses did accompany him with his hawks and spaniels." Canon Jackson relates that Aubrey was on his way to visit Sir James at Draycot, when he died at Oxford. Sir James Long married Dorothy, daughter of Sir Edward Leach of Shipley. By her he had a

[1] Falcon holders.   [2] Labels.

THE KEEPER'S LODGE, DRAYCOT PARK.

son called James, who died before his father, leaving
a son also called James. So when Sir James Long
died in 1691 his grandson succeeded to the title and
estates. He died in 1729, when his son Robert
inherited Draycot. Sir Robert was afterwards M.P.
for Wootton Bassett. He married in 1735 Lady
Emma Child, the only daughter of John, first Earl
of Tylney. This lady, who brought so much wealth
into the Long family, was directly descended from
Sir Josiah Child, the second son of Richard Child,
Esq., Merchant of London, who was descended
from the ancient family of Childs, for many years
seated at Northwick Poole, Shrowley and Pencock,
County Worcester. Sir Josiah Child was an Alder-
man, an eminent Merchant of London, sometime
Governor of the East India Company, and the
Founder of Child's Bank. He attained to great
wealth, was thrice married, and by each of his wives
had one or more children, who married into some of
the highest families of the nobility. His last wife
Emma, youngest daughter and co-heiress of Sir
Henry Bernard of Stoke, Salop, and widow of Sir
Thomas Willoughby, died in 1735, having survived
her second husband, Sir Josiah, thirty-six years.
About this lady we are told by Mount, the historian
of Essex : " It is said she was nearly allied to so
many of the prime nobility, that eleven Dukes and
Duchesses used to ask her blessing, and it was

reckoned that above fifty great families would go into mourning for her." Sir Josiah was created a baronet the 18th July, 1678, and died the 22nd June, 1699.

Richard, the grandson of Sir Josiah Child, was the third Baronet. He married Dorothy, daughter and heiress of John Glynne, Esq., of Henley Park, Surrey. This Mr. Glynne came into possession of the Tylney estate through his wife, the daughter and heiress of Francis Tylney, Esq., of Tylney Hall, in the parish of Rotherwick, Hants. She was also named Dorothy. Sir Richard Child was created, by George the First, Baron of Newtown and Viscount Castlemaine. He expended a portion of his great wealth in building the magnificent mansion of Wanstead, in Essex. The erection of this princely residence cost £360,000. It was reckoned, in some ways, a palace superior to Blenheim or Houghton. In 1731 Sir Richard, or rather Baron, Newtown, was made Earl of Tylney by George the Second, taking his title from his wife's property of Tylney Hall.[1] In 1734 an Act of Parliament was passed enabling Lord Tylney's eldest son, John, and his heirs to bear the surname of Tylney, in consequence of an estate of £7,000 a year which he inherited through his mother, Countess Tylney.

John, second Earl of Tylney, never married, so

[1] Tylney Hall was rebuilt in 1879. It is close to the site of the old Hall, and is now the seat of Lionel Phillips, Esq.

his only sister, Lady Emma Child, was his heiress presumptive. She was married in 1735 to Sir Robert Long, by whom she had eight children.

I have often looked at the picture of this beautiful woman in Lady Victoria Wellesley's collection of family portraits. The portrait represents her in an evening dress of rich white satin. Her hair is drawn back from her forehead and dressed high. Her face has a very sweet expression, and her dark eyes look steadfastly at you. Lady Emma died in 1758. Sir Robert survived his beautiful wife nine years. There are letters still extant which show the great affection which existed between Earl Tylney, his brother-in-law, Sir Robert Long, and his nephew and heir, James, whom he familiarly called Jemmy Long. These letters passed frequently, for those days, between Draycot and Wanstead. In June, 1760, Lord Tylney thus writes to his brother-in-law : " I give you leave to guess the confusion I must be in, when that I acquaint you that the Duke of York sent last night that he intends doing me the honour to sup at Wanstead next Monday, and, of course, must have a ball. The little notice he has given me will make it very difficult for me to get company suitable for H.R.H. the Duke of York." He then goes on to express the hope " that ' Jemmy Long ' will be of the party."

This eldest son of Sir Robert Long seems to have

B

been a great favourite in his family. It is quite a lesson on the duty to parents to read the letters which were written by him and his sisters to their father.   While taking a tour abroad in 1763, James Long always addressed him as " Dear Sir," and signed himself " Your dutiful Son."

When Sir Robert Long died, in 1767, his son James came into his title and the Draycot Estates. The two next sons had died young.

The fourth son, Charles Long, of Grittleton, Hants, had married a daughter of Thomas Phipps, Esq. From their daughter Emma, the Powlett Scropes, a well-known family in Wiltshire, are descended. Sir Robert's two daughters, Dorothy and Emma, died unmarried.   Lord Tylney died in 1784, a long time after his sister and presumptive heiress Lady Emma Long.

With Lord Tylney's death, without male heirs direct, the Earldom of Tylney and his other titles became extinct.   His vast fortune and princely estate of Wanstead, together with the Tylney property, passed to his eldest nephew, Sir James Long of Draycot, the son of his only sister, Lady Emma Long.

Wanstead[1] House was a very large and magnificent structure, standing in an extensive park,

---

[1] On June 20th, 1624, Archbishop Usher preached before James the First at Wanstead.

and surrounded by gardens and pleasure grounds.
The principal front was two hundred and sixty
feet in length. The entrance was in the centre,
beneath a grand portico of six Corinthian columns,
having a flight of steps on each side, and in
the tympanum the arms of the Tylney family
finely sculptured. The garden front had a pedi-
ment enriched with a bas-relief, and supported by
six three-quarter columns. The whole building
was cased with Portland stone, and its depth was
between seventy and eighty feet. It consisted of
two stories, the uppermost containing the ball-room,
state bed-chambers, and other principal apartments.
Over the door, leading into the great hall, was a
medallion of Colin Campbell, the architect, who
achieved great and deserved reputation, owing to
the science and judgment displayed by him in
the construction of the edifice. The hall, fifty-
one feet by thirty-six, was decorated in all the
splendour of the last age. The ceiling was gilt, and
was painted by Trent, there being personifications
on it of morning, noon, evening, and night. The
walls were ornamented with paintings from Roman
history by Cassati, representing Coriolanus and his
mother, Porsenna, and Pompey's last interview with
his family. There was also a portrait of Trent, who
painted several ceilings there besides that of the
hall. There were, moreover, two large statues,

brought from the ruins of Herculaneum, one of Bonntian, the other of Livia, Agrippa's wife. Several suites of rooms extended from each side of the hall, comprising, among others, a ball-room, a saloon, and four spacious and well proportioned bed-chambers. The ball-room, seventy-five feet by twenty-seven, was magnificently fitted with all the luxurious accessories of the last century, the furniture being richly embossed and the walls hung with tapestry. The latter was well executed, and represented the story of Telemachus, and the battles of Alexander in two compartments. Over the chimney piece there was a fine painting of Portia, the wife of Brutus, by Schulken. The saloon, thirty feet square, was highly embellished and contained several statues, also a picture of Pandora, by Nolleskins, father of the eminent sculptor of that name. In the bedrooms were various paintings, among them St. John and the Virgin, by Raphael; Apollo and Narcissus; Cupid, by Correggio; Venus sleeping; Venus and Adonis; Cupid and Psyche; Diana and Endymion; besides several views.

The principal dining-room, forty feet by twenty-seven, was embellished with paintings by Cassati, representing Sophonisba taking poison, and Alexander directing Appelles to paint Campespe. The apartments also contained several good

landscapes and views of famous ruins. Various
paintings were distributed through the other
rooms. The best of these were St. Francis
and the Holy Family, by Guido; Herodias, with
the head of John the Baptist, supposed to be
by Titian; some flower pieces by Baptiste; Lord
Chief Justice Glynn and his family, by Lely;
and Sir Josiah Child. On the ceiling of one of
the drawing-rooms was a painting of Jupiter, and in
the centre of the chimney piece was the family crest
of the Tylneys, a flying eagle with a snake in white
marble. The prospects from several of the apartments were extremely beautiful, and included a very
extensive range of the surrounding country. From
the entrance to the park on the west, the road to
the house was skirted by rows of fine elms. This
pathway winds round a circular piece of water,
extending considerably beyond either extremity of
the mansion, which, as viewed from the approach,
had an aspect of much grandeur. The gardens and
pleasure grounds were laid out, prior to the building
of the house, by Sir Richard Child. Opposite the
back front there was an easy ascent, through a
pleasant vista, to the river Moding, which is formed
into canals, and had near it a curious grotto, which
was constructed by the second Earl Tylney, at
an expenditure of £2,000, exclusive of its costly
materials. The slopes, or elevated grounds, border-

ing the river, were planted with trees, as were also various parts of the estate. On the south side of the park, nearly adjoining the grounds at Aldersbrook, a tesselated pavement was discovered, in the year 1735, by some labourers, who were engaged in digging holes to plant an avenue of trees brought from the gardens. Its extent, from north to south, was about 20 feet, and from east to west some 16 feet. The tesseræ were of brick, of various sizes and colours. On the outside they were red, forming a border, of about a foot in breadth, within which were several ornaments, and in the centre the figure of a man mounted on a beast, whose identity could not be decided with certainty. A small brass coin of the Emperor Valens, a silver coin, and several large pieces of Roman brick, were also discovered among the ruins.

Mr. Lethicullier surmised that these remains originally formed the pavement of a banqueting room of a villa. About three hundred yards further, on the south, ruins of brick, foundations have been met with, as also fragments of urns, Roman coins and other antiquities.[1]

I am told by the Rev. Prebendary Lunt, who was at one time Rector of Leyton, the adjoining parish to Wanstead, that some evidences of this once

---

[1] This account of Wanstead is taken from a paper read at the Leyton Club by Edward James Elliott.

WANSTEAD HOUSE, ESSEX.

magnificent mansion are still to be seen. There are yet the remains of garden and pleasure ground. The beautiful terraces are still there, as well as the lake, which once formed so striking a feature in the grounds.

When Sir James Long came into possession of Wanstead, it may be said that the prosperity of the Draycot Longs had reached its zenith. In 1785, Sir James Tylney Long still further added to the Draycot property by purchasing Seagry from the Houltons. Seagry possesses a Manor House of its own. It is not far from Draycot, and so it must have seemed a desirable place to annex to the estate. Sir James also stood M.P. for Wilts. He married first Harriett, fourth daughter of Viscount Folkstone. She died in 1777, leaving no children. He married, secondly, Lady Catherine Sidney Windsor, daughter of Otho, fourth Earl of Plymouth. The ancient seat of the Earls of Plymouth was Warmstry House, Worcester.

I found the following account of this mansion in Binns' " History of Worcester Pottery ": " Having resolved upon establishing a manufactory for porcelain, the first requirement, after the invention of a body, would be a suitable locality. This presented itself at once in the premises known by the name of Warmstry House, formerly the residence of the Windsor family. The building thus selected deserves some notice at our hands. It will be found marked on all the old maps of the city. It was formerly a large and handsome mansion, with gardens laid out down to the banks of the river. The house forms a sort of quadrangle, with a court in the centre, and is conjectured to have been occupied as far back as the reign of Henry the Seventh by Sir William Windsor, an ancestor of the Earls of Plymouth. On the first floor was a parlour wainscotted round with oak, and over the fireplace a curious armorial design carved in wood, and bearing the marks of great age. They were the arms of William, second Lord Windsor, and such as were borne by the Earls of Plymouth. Lady Catherine Sidney Windsor was married to Sir James Tylney Long on July 25th, 1785. They resided for many years at Draycot Cerne, which was their favourite place. Theirs was, in all respects, a happy marriage. Their tastes and feelings were the same. Sir James was a generous promoter of public and private charities; the latter, in particular, at once gratified his feelings and occupied his mind. Volumes might be filled in describing his benevolence. In the three adjoining parishes to Draycot he instituted both a Sunday and a Day School, and he and Lady Catherine took great interest in distributing the prizes to the children. In those days schools were comparatively scarce. The Government had not turned its attention to the education of the poor, and their well-being, in this respect, was vested in private hands. In winter the poor in the neighbour-hood of their different residences were supplied with weekly portions, and the aged and infirm comfortably clothed. Lady Catherine directed her benevolence not only to the aged and infirm. Wherever she found those who had known better days, and were reduced by misfortune, to them she became a bene-factress and a kind and generous friend. Instances of her liberality, in such cases, have been known that would have done honour to the fortune of a prince."

Blest with such a wife, Sir James passed seven years in complete happiness with her. Their tastes, their pursuits and their inclinations were completely similar. It seemed as if one soul actuated the move-ments of their separate frames, and it was difficult to say whether the mild influence of benevolence oper-ated with greater force upon the husband or the wife.

As to the birth of their first child, Catherine, after-wards the heiress of Wanstead, celebrated alike for her wealth and her misfortunes, a curious incident occurred, which like many so-called accidental cir-cumstances, bore its after prints. Sir James and Lady Catherine Long were posting from London to Draycot, with the intention of their heir being born in the ancestral home of the Longs. However, when they reached a small country town, a little distance from Chippenham, Lady Catherine was suddenly

taken ill, and they had to stop at the nearest inn.
The first doctor who could be found was hastily
called in.   His name was John Barry, afterwards
of 7, Burlington Street, Bath, and then in practice
at Chippenham.   Under his care their first-born
child, (who was to be Lady Victoria Wellesley's
mother), was brought into the world.   Their acquaintance with John Barry did not end with this.   He
afterwards became a cherished friend, and, in finan-
cial matters, a clever adviser.   He was afterwards
trustee to Lady Catherine's will, and his love and
care for the Tylney Long family only ended with
his death.   I have often heard his youngest daughter,
(Mrs. Stone, of Sydney House, Bath) speak of her
pleasant remembrances of visits with her father
spent at Draycot House, and of the kindness they
received there.

   Two more daughters were afterwards born, named,
like their aunts, Dorothy and Emma.   But the one
drawback to their happiness was the want of a male
heir to those vast estates.   However, in the ninth year
of their married life, just after a serious illness of Sir
James, which lasted two years, a little son was born.
With Sir James's recovered health, and the arrival of
an heir, their happiness seemed complete.   But in
1794 Sir James expired, leaving his three daughters
and his infant son, too young to know the nature of
their loss.

After a time of almost inconsolable grief, Lady Catherine applied herself with vigour to her maternal duties. The health of the young Baronet, the infant Sir James, had always been delicate, and repeated fears agitated his mother's mind. The family physician gave it as his opinion that he was fostered with too great a degree of care, and that his constitution would be strengthened by the regular system adopted at school. Lady Catherine took this advice, and, accordingly, to school this precious boy was sent. For a time his health seemed improved, but not for long. He died in 1805, in his eleventh year. The end of his little life closed an important chapter in the history of his family. By his death the Baronetcy became extinct, and his eldest sister, Catherine, inherited his fortune and estates.

Wiltshire abounds with relics of the ancient family of Long. In the Church at Box two old tombs were found, one of Anthony Long in 1578, the other of Jewell Long in 1647.

The use of the fetterlock in the coats of arms in the Churches of South Wraxall, Priston, Draycot, and other places, has been a subject of much discussion. Some have held that the Cernes used it from one of their family having been present at the King's coronation ; others assert that it was used by the Longs fifty years before they had any connection with the Cernes.

CHAPTER III.

The Heiress of Wanstead.

BY the will of Sir James Tylney Long, his eldest daughter Catherine was made heiress to her brother. When, therefore, the young Baronet died, Lady Catherine had the great responsibility of taking care of the richest heiress in the kingdom, with her rent roll of forty thousand a year. Many were the suitors who tried for the hand of the wealthy Miss Tylney Long, but for a time they tried in vain. So eager was the contest as to who should win this charming but extremely *petite* heiress, that the following parody on Pope's lines was written and published :—

> " Man wants but little here below,
> But wants that little Long."

At last, like the Lady of the Leal, Miss Tylney Long's heart was won. Mr. Pole Wellesley, son of Lord Maryborough, and nephew of the great Duke of Wellington, with his fascinating manners, succeeded in winning the hand of the heiress, and she became engaged to him.

The marriage of the Hon. William Pole Wellesley with the Heiress of Wanstead and Draycot was solemnized at St. James' Church, Piccadilly, on Saturday, March 14th, 1812. They were married, as was the custom in those days, by special license. A newspaper of that date gives the following account :—

" The long talked of matrimonial alliance between Mr. Pole, now Wellesley, and Miss Tylney Long, took place on Saturday evening. The parties met at Lord Montgomerie's house in Hamilton Place, Piccadilly, at five o'clock, and about six, accompanied by many of their nearest relations, they went, in Lady Catherine Long's coach, to St. James' Church, in Piccadilly. The Marquis of Wellesley handed Miss Long out of the carriage and conducted her through the rector's house (Dr. Andrews) to the Altar of Hymen. There were present at the ceremony, which was performed by Dr. Glasse, Rector of Wanstead, Mr. Secretary Pole, Lady Catherine Long, Miss Dora Long, and Miss Emma Long. The two latter were bridesmaids. The usual forms being gone through, the happy couple retired by the southern gate, which leads through the churchyard into Jermyn Street, where a new and magnificent equipage was in waiting to receive them. It was a

singularly elegant chariot, painted bright yellow,
and highly emblazoned, and drawn by four beautiful
Arabian grey horses, attended by two postillions in
brown jackets, with superb emblazoned badges in
gold, emblematic of the united arms of the Wellesley
and Tylney families. The newly married pair drove
off, with great speed, for Blackheath, intending to
pass the night at the tasteful chateau belonging to
the bridegroom's father, and from thence proceed
to Wanstead House, in Essex, on the following day,
to pass the honeymoon. The bride's dress exceeded
in costliness and beauty the celebrated dress worn
by Lady Morpeth at the time of her marriage, which
was exhibited for a fortnight at least, by her mother,
the late Duchess of Devonshire. The dress of the
present bride consisted of a robe of real Brussels
point lace, the device a simple sprig; it was placed
over white satin. Her head was ornamented with a
cottage bonnet of the same material, being Brussels
lace with two ostrich feathers. She likewise wore
a deep lace veil and a white satin pelisse trimmed
with swansdown. The dress cost seven hundred
guineas, the bonnet one hundred and fifty, and the
veil two hundred, and she wore a necklace which
cost £25,000. Mr. Pole wore a plain blue coat with
yellow buttons, a white waistcoat and buff breeches,
and white silk stockings. It was to elude the eager
curiosity of the crowd, that they retired from the

Church by the door opposite to the one at which they had entered. Yesterday the wedding favours were distributed among their numerous friends (the number exceeded eight hundred), composed wholly of silver, and unique in form, those for the ladies having an acorn in the centre, and the gentlemen's a star; each cost a guinea and a half. The inferior ones, for domestics and others, were made of white satin ribbon, with silver stars and silver balls and fringe.

" Every domestic in the family of Lady Catherine Long has been liberally provided for; they all have had annuities settled upon them, and Mrs. Tylney Long Wellesley's own waiting woman, who was nurse to her in her infancy, has been liberally considered. The income remaining to Mrs. Tylney Long Wellesley, after allowing for considerable sums given as an additional portion to each of the Misses Long and an annuity to Lady Catherine, is £80,000 per annum."

The sum spoken of is somewhat exaggerated. But what fortune, however vast, is not exaggerated ! In Lady Victoria's own handwriting, her mother's income is put down as £40,000. Her history will show how very little of the sums set apart for younger children, was realized by her as Mrs. Tylney Long Wellesley's only daughter. Upon his marriage Mr. Pole Wellesley assumed the name and arms of the Tylney Longs, in addition to his own.

As was observed in a newspaper of later date: "The Hon. gentleman's married life was entered upon under the very happiest auspices, auspices which should have been the forerunners of anything but the misery and ruin that ensued. For the first eleven years of their married life, Mr. and Mrs. Long Wellesley lived together on very affectionate terms. Their first child, William Richard Arthur, afterwards fifth Earl of Mornington, was born at Wanstead House, October 7th, 1813. Then followed the birth of their second son, James Fitzroy Henry, in 1815. On the 29th of May, 1818, their third child and only daughter, Victoria Catherine Mary, was born also at Wanstead House. On the 2nd of June she was privately baptized by the Rev. William Gilly, Rector of Wanstead. Later on she was publicly received into the Church by the same clergyman. About the time of her birth, Mr. Long Wellesley stood for the borough. He said, that if he succeeded in being elected M.P., he would name his little daughter Victory. So that was how she received her name of Victoria, not, as some have thought, from any connection with the Queen, whose senior she was by one year. In 1822, Mr. and Mrs. Long Wellesley left England and resided in different places on the Continent. In a letter from Miss Emma Tylney Long to her sister, dated Draycot,

September 19th, 1822, she writes as if she thought
her fairly happy.   Though some troubles are alluded
to, they are considered as passed by.   She writes :
" I hope your valuable life will be prolonged through
many happy years.   As to Mr. L. W. he now
knows your worth and is, of course, anxious to
preserve such a blessing, as he feels you are, to himself and the dear children."   Mrs. Long Wellesley
was then with her husband and children at Calais,
en route for Geneva.   Lady Catherine Long was
at that time residing with her two other daughters
at Draycot, which seems to have been left to her for
life.   Throughout this year, the health of Lady
Catherine Long began to fail, and very anxious
letters were dispatched by the Misses Long from
Draycot to Mrs. Long Wellesley abroad.   A letter
from her youngest sister, Emma, dated November
25th, speaks of her mother as better.   She alludes
to the eldest boy (afterwards Lord Mornington)
having fallen into the Lake of Geneva and hopes he
will not also fall into the Bay of Naples.

Another letter from her eldest sister, Dora, on
December 19th, speaks also of her mother as better,
and adds this pleasing testimony to her worth :
" Allowing for her infirmities, who has spent their
time more excellently than this dear creature, in
doing all the good in her power without ostentation,
but with inspiring benevolence, instilling good prin-

c

ciples into her children, her servants, and neighbours.
All her pursuits have been pure and innocent."

Miss Long goes on to add that their dear mother
had been in some anxiety, lest her grandchildren's
seeing so much of the world so early in life, might
tend to weaken their religious impressions ; but that
she had consoled her by telling her that their mother
had sent to England for religious books, written
specially for the use of the young.

A letter, dated Naples, December 1st, 1822, from
Mrs. Long Wellesley to her sister Dora, expresses
much anxiety about Lady Catherine's health. She
writes that she is enjoying Naples, though it was
bitterly cold, and snow had fallen upon the mountains.   She was anxious about her husband, who
had been unwell with low fever.   The letter was
that of a happy wife and mother.   In it she said,
" You say you hope we are all well, and happy, and
comfortable.   Indeed, with the exception of his
being so unwell, which I think will be of short
duration, I have every reason to be so."   Of her
little girl, who was then four years old, she writes :
" The dear baby has entirely got rid of the eruption,
but her hair has become so weak that I think, when
the weather is warmer, I shall have it shaved.   Mrs.
Gordon has given her a beautiful present of a box of
bonbons, as a Christmas box.   She has also received
a very pretty doll from Mrs. Prince, and a work-bag

from Captain Schonberg, who commands the Roch-
fort. She is in high favour with everybody here."
Perhaps it was owing to her mother's early attention
that Lady Victoria afterwards had such an abundant and beautiful head of hair.

In the beginning of the year 1823, Lady Catherine
Long passed away. She died on Sunday, January
5th. It was a sad event for all who knew her.
Amongst the villagers of Draycot, by whom she was
colloquially called Lady Kattern, her loss was severely
felt, for to them she had ever been a true and kind
friend.

A newspaper of the time thus writes of her:
" Lady Catherine Tylney Long may, assuredly, be
considered to have been one of the highest ornaments
of the age in which she lived. She was distinguished
by her sweetness of temper, mildness of demeanour,
her love of domestic life, and her almost un-
paralleled benevolence."

In another paper this notice appeared: " The
loss of this excellent lady will long be deplored by
all who had the honour of her acquaintance, but by
none more than the poor of her neighbourhood, to
whom she was a very munificent benefactress."

In a letter, dated Naples, February 4th, 1823,
Mrs. Long Wellesley expressed to her sister Dora
" her heartfelt pain at hearing the sad, sad news,
that their excellent mother was no more. This,"

she writes, " is indeed a trial, but we must bear it
with fortitude and resignation.   It is the will of God,
and we must submit."   Then, after expressing the
most affectionate solicitude for her sisters, she
adds :—

  " I have received the greatest kindness and affection
from Mr. L. W.   No human creature could have
been more kind, or shown greater feeling upon the
sad occasion, than he has done.   The dear eldest,
too, has been most affectionate.   I hope you have
received the letter which Mr. L. W. wrote to you
on the 31st.   He tells me he has written to you again
to-day, in case the letter he wrote on Friday should
not get to you safely.   I saw a most kind letter he
wrote yesterday to Lord Maryborough, in which he
desires him strictly to attend to your wishes in
everything.   I am very sorry you think of going
from Draycot, but I hope it will only be for a short
time, and that after the change at Clifton you will
return there until our return, which will not be
before August.

  " God bless you, my dear Dora.

          " Believe me ever,

                  " Affectionately yours,

                          " C. LONG WELLESLEY."

  In those days letters took three weeks to reach
Naples from England.   The cost of postage was
two shillings and sixpence, which was paid by the

recipient. In reply to Mrs. Long Wellesley's letter, her sister writes : " What gratitude we feel to Mr. L. W. for his affectionate attentions to you in your distress. I am sure his own heart must have urged him to do all in his power towards its alleviation, and thus to repay you for your generous devotion to him upon those trying occasions."

An offer of Seagry House, near Draycot, having been made by Mr. Long Wellesley as the future residence of his wife's sisters, Miss Long thus expresses herself to her brother-in-law in a letter dated February 27th, 1823 : " I cannot express how we feel obliged to you for actually thinking so very much about us as to have given us the choice of a residence, in every point of view most desirable, with the offer of Draycot for our present accommodation. Nothing, certainly, could be more considerate of our interests as such conduct, but we decline your obliging proposal with a thousand thanks. It is our intention to be travelling about."

CHAPTER IV.

"None so Sad as She."

S to the later part of Mrs. Long Wellesley's married life, the sorrows she went through were matters of history in the time in which she lived.

The patience and long-suffering with which she bore them are shown alike by her private letters and by the admiration of her expressed by her friends. But let "the dead past bury its dead." We will draw a veil over facts too sad to dwell upon, and feelings too sacred to record.

Soon after Lady Catherine Long's death in 1823, Mr. Long Wellesley decided that Wanstead House was too expensive a place to keep up, and that it must be taken down. How Mrs. Long Wellesley's consent was gained for the sad destruction of this beautiful house does not appear. The little Victoria first felt a touch of the sorrows of life when she was three years old. In 1823, when her grandmother died, and later in that same year, when Wanstead House was taken down, she was but five years old. Her keen memory could, however, go back to that early date, when she first realized that her mother was sorrowful.

The wealth, which had for so long enriched the Tylney Longs, was fast passing away. For, in eleven years, Mr. Pole Wellesley's extravagance had so seriously impaired his wife's vast fortune that Wanstead, (a palace superior in some ways to Blenheim and Houghton), had to be sacrificed. This splendid mansion, the erection of which had cost £360,000, was taken down and sold to a Norwich builder for £10,000, upon the condition that every vestige of the magnificent fabric, even the foundations, should be removed within the following twelve months.

In 1824, Mrs. Long Wellesley returned to England, and with her husband's consent, went with her three children to reside at Draycot House. Before leaving Paris, she received a letter from Mr. Long Wellesley, concerning his wishes as to the management of their two boys and their little daughter, Victoria. Whatever were Mr. Long Wellesley's faults he was a fond father, for in this letter he adds: " It breaks my heart to part with my children."

Mrs. Long Wellesley wrote him a few pathetic lines in reply, saying she could not leave Paris with-

out thanking him for allowing her to have the care
of their children, and that she would attend to his
injunctions concerning them.

Shortly afterwards, Mr. Long Wellesley sent for
his two boys, leaving the little girl, then six years
old, with Mrs. Long Wellesley at Draycot. So,
separated from her brothers, the child enlivened her
mother's solitude, or played alone in the halls of
Draycot and in the beautiful gardens around. The
old clerk, Giddins, was a special favourite and play-
mate of the little Victoria. He was one of the
celebrities of the quiet village. He was a ponderous man, almost a giant in height and size. It was
the little girl's great delight to make this big man
sit in one of the arbours and drink tea with her out
of her set of doll's tea-things. It was considered a
most amusing sight to see this enormous man sitting by the side of the fairy-like child, and holding the
tiny tea-cup in his ponderous hand. In a letter,
dated Draycot House, May 2nd, 1825, Mrs. Long
Wellesley wrote a long and affectionate letter to her
sister Emma. This letter is written in the calm
tone of one who has accepted her sad lot, and
achieved a temporary tranquility of feeling. For
some reason not explained, the little Victoria was,
at that time, taken care of by Mrs. Long Wellesley's
sisters. She does not feel assured as to having her
altogether in the future, but hopes that an order

from the Lord Chancellor may enable her to do so.
. She writes that she fears to remove her dear little
girl lest it should be wrong in the eyes of the law.
She mentions kind letters received from Sir George
Dallas and Dr. Gladstone, full of feeling for herself
and her dear little angel. She says that she has
decided on taking a house in London, and adds how
she longs to see her dear sisters, and to have the
society of her dear little girl, but is ready to give up
anything for the child's ultimate good.

A little time after the date of this letter Mrs. Long
Wellesley left Draycot, never to see it again, and
settled in the house she had taken at 41, Clarges
Street. Here, with a breaking heart and failing
health, she could only have resided a few months.
As she became weaker and more depressed, it
seemed necessary she should be under the immediate
care of her relatives. So on Wednesday, the 7th of
September, the Misses Tylney Long removed, with
their unhappy sister and her children, to a house in
the Paragon, Richmond. She had previously been
much indisposed. On the evening of the 7th she
was seized with spasms, which occasioned her so
much alarm that she called her sister Dora into
another room and told her that, as spasms in the
stomach often proved fatal, she considered it her
duty to revoke, without delay, a will she had made
some years before, probably in 1815, under Mr. Long

Wellesley's direction. Although she did not recollect the particulars of it, she suspected it might be unfavourable to the interests of her children. She then wrote a short revocation of that will, and signed it in the presence of two witnesses, Mr. John Pitman and Henry Bicknell. Immediately after her sister Emma entered her room ; upon which she showed her the paper, saying, " See what I have signed." Miss Emma Long then read the paper. After this Mrs. Long Wellesley deposited it in her portfolio, and proceeded into an adjoining room to consult Dr. Julius relative to her indisposition. He prescribed a medicine, and the spasms subsided. She afterwards gave particular directions respecting her children's sleeping apartments. On the evening of the next day Mrs. Long Wellesley was seized with a fit of hysterics. On the following Friday week she was so far well as to be able to walk out. However, she soon became rapidly worse, and on Monday, September 12th, 1825, she died somewhat suddenly at eleven o'clock in the morning. This was only nine days after her arrival at Richmond. She was attended in her last illness by Sir H. Dundas. Her three children were too young to know their loss. Her eldest son, William, was only ten years old, her next son, James Fitzroy, eight, and her only daughter, Victoria, but seven years old.

Some verses to her memory were written by Sir

George Dallas, and accompanied with this touching
heading :—

AN EPITAPH.

SACRED TO THE MEMORY OF

THE HONOURABLE MRS. LONG WELLESLEY,

who, confessing the redeeming merits of an atoning Saviour,
sustained by faith and hope, and dying of a broken heart,
departed this life, after a short illness of only three days, on
the 12th of September, 1825, in the thirty-fifth year of
her age.

An all-gracious Providence, rewarding the piety and purity
of her life, and commiserating the misfortunes which so sadly
closed it, mercifully removed her from this tearful vale, to
enjoy in a brighter sphere that happiness of which she had
been deprived in this world, and which she had uniformly
endeavoured to deserve by a constant exercise of the most
exemplary virtues. Few of her sex ever commenced life with
more brilliant prospects, or closed it under a darker cloud.

Nature endowed her with mental and personal attractions,
which in themselves would have given lustre to minor possessions, but thus doubly enriched, she became an early object
of pursuit and general admiration. Her hand was sought by
the proudest and richest peers of the land. In her was
centred every quality that could bless and render man happy,
a temper mild and serene, a mind calm and sensible, manners
polished and graceful, affections devoted and constant, a
breast wherein the virtues seemed to have fixed their abode,
and a heart overflowing with the kindest sympathies of human
nature. In the relative duties of daughter, sister, wife and
mother, she exhibited a bright example of whatever could
dignify her sex and exalt it to general admiration. The shafts
of envy never reached her. The voice of slander never

assailed her. In an age of dissipation she shunned its follies,
and sought, in the shade of domestic retirement, to rear her
children to the virtues she practised. Those who knew her
can attest the wakeful fondness with which she watched over
their rising innocence, and endeavoured to shape it with the
safeguard of those religious principles which, early impressed,
become the steps to temporal and eternal happiness. Her
last sigh was for them, and the names of William, James and
Victoria, hung lingering on her quivering lips as the faint and
protracted echoes of her last thoughts.

It was stated in a newspaper of the time that the
"death of this lamented lady excites a great degree
of interest in the fashionable world."

The following notice of her funeral appeared :—

"On Monday morning last, at the hour of nine
o'clock, the remains of this unfortunate lady
left Richmond for the family mansion at Draycot, and arrived there on Thursday. The procession consisted of the hearse in which the coffin
was borne, drawn by six horses, and three mourning
coaches drawn by four horses each. The chief
mourners were the two Misses Long, Lord Maryborough, the Duke of Wellington and some other
relations. Within half a mile of Draycot the funeral
procession was joined by thirty-two of the tenants
in black cloaks and on horseback. All the inhabitants of the village appeared in mourning. The
Church was hung in black, and on the front of the
pulpit were the family arms. The funeral was con-

ducted by Messrs. Banting, the King's upholsterers, Pall Mall."

Thus passed away, from earthly wealth and from earthly sorrow, the richest heiress in England (at that time) and the mother of the future Lady Victoria Long Wellesley.

The Age, a newspaper of the day, said of her in an account of her death: " To her no luxury could be a novelty, no society an elevation ; for her halls had sheltered the Princes of other lands in adversity, and feasted those of her own country in prosperity. She stood, therefore, in the world an enviable and an envied woman."

CHAPTER V.

The Iron Duke and his Young Wards.

SOON after Mrs. Long Wellesley's death, letters full of feeling were received by Miss Long from Lord and Lady Maryborough. The former writes: "I have had nothing more at heart than showing my respect and affection for that exemplary and suffering angel."

Poor Lady Maryborough wrote thus: "The late events have broken my heart, nor do I see a prospect of anything like peace or comfort. I only wonder, with admiration, at the Christian meekness and forbearance you have shown, and which, I am sure, nothing but the piety in which you were all brought up could have effected. I wish the dear children were thoroughly secure. So long as that dear little Victoria is with you her health is taken care of. From her tender years she will not be sensible of the irreparable loss she has sustained. But if anything occurs to drag her from you, I am afraid for her health, for she never appeared to me very strong."

On the 28th of September, Miss Long wrote a
confidential letter to Lord Maryborough, in which
she expressed her and her sister's heartfelt satisfaction that he and Lady Maryborough were so anxious
to fulfil the last wishes of their beloved sister. This
was in allusion to the steps which Mrs. Long
Wellesley had taken, just before her death, to make
them wards of Chancery. In case Mr. Long
Wellesley should claim the custody of the children,
she (Miss Long) felt she could not more effectually
forward the views of their poor mother than by
instantly taking steps for constituting them wards
in Chancery. She reminded Lord Maryborough
that, by her father's will, a power was given to her
late sister to charge the estates with portions of
£3,000 each in favour of her younger children, to
take effect from the period of her death. Miss
Long therefore considered that, having this property,
the younger children, as well as the eldest boy, were
subjects for the protection of the Court of Chancery.
She informed Lord Maryborough that Mr. Long
Wellesley had given orders for all three of the children to be sent over to him, but that she and her
sister had ventured to resist that order, upon the
plea that, being wards of Chancery, they might not
be removed out of the country without the permission
of the Lord Chancellor. Miss Long added : " I need
not say how very anxious we are to have your and

Lady Maryborough's continued countenance and approbation of all that has been done relative to your grandchildren. Indeed, what can we desire more than the approbation of those who possessed my dear sister's unlimited confidence, and from whose kindness and affection she derived the greatest consolation under her trials."

Miss Long went on to remind Lord Maryborough of a power which her sister possessed of disposing by will of £50,000; of the will she had executed under her husband's directions; of the paper revoking that will, which she had signed shortly before her death, and of her fears lest that paper may be disputed as informal.

Judging from after events, Miss Long's fears were only too well founded. For £3,000 was the sum eventually spoken of as the portion of the only daughter of the richest heiress in the kingdom. After much anxiety and trouble on the part of the Misses Long and their friends, it became the decision of Lord Eldon, who was then Lord Chancellor, that the children of Mr. and Mrs. Long Wellesley should all be entrusted to their mother's relatives, and entirely removed from their father's care. Such a decision, that a father should not be allowed the care of his own sons, was at that time without precedent in the history of the law.

Miss Long, anxious to secure the Duke of Wellington as guardian to the children, then wrote to him in these terms :—

> "*Elizabeth House, Hampstead,*
> "*November,* 1825.

"The very delicate situation in which Mr. Long Wellesley has placed Lord Maryborough, having obliged him to decline accepting the office of guardian to the children of our lamented sister, Mrs. Long Wellesley, we are induced to solicit from your Grace the very great favour of taking on yourself this protective office, and of permitting us to associate your name with that of our uncle, Colonel Windsor, in the trust. We conceive that your Grace's acceptance of this trust would give great satisfaction to Mr. Long Wellesley and family, and we feel deeply how gratifying it would be to ourselves. Should you feel disposed to undertake the office we beg to assure you that both Colonel Windsor and ourselves will feel happy to relieve your Grace from *much* of the trouble.

> "I have the honour to be,
> "D. T. LONG.

"His Grace the Duke of Wellington."

The Duke, having consented to undertake the office of guardian, confirmed his consent in the two following letters :—

D

" *London,*
" *December 2nd,* 1825.

" My dear Madam,—I have received your letter, and I will wait upon you, either on Sunday afternoon, or on Monday, to converse with you on the future disposal of the children.

" I think we understand each other perfectly. First, I will zealously, and to the best of my abilities, execute the trust to be reposed in me by the Lord Chancellor, as the guardian of the children, for their benefit and welfare, and in opposition to all mankind. Secondly, to the question of guardian or no guardian I have nothing to say, that rests entirely between their father on the one hand, and the family of their lamented mother on the other.

" But thirdly, till the Chancellor will decide that the guardianship is at an end, I will continue to perform the duties of guardian to the best of my abilites.

" Believe me, my dear Madam,
" Ever yours most faithfully,
" WELLINGTON."

" *Teddesley,*
" *December 9th,* 1825.

" My dear Miss Long,—I received this morning your letter of the ——, in which you inform me of Colonel Windsor's intention of calling upon me on

Thursday. I left London on Wednesday, and am very sorry that I could not have the pleasure of meeting him.

" In consequence, however, of what you tell me of his opinion regarding Eton School, I will immediately write to Mr. Hawtrey and enquire whether he can receive the boys and their tutor; we will, of course, settle nothing till I shall have had an opportunity of communicating with Colonel Windsor.

" I will let you know the result of my communication with Mr. Hawtrey.

" Ever yours, my dear Madam,
" Most faithfully,
" WELLINGTON."

Some mistake as to what the Duke had said having occurred, he wrote in the following terms to Miss Long :—

" *London*,
" *May* 23rd, 1826.

" My dear Madam,—I enclose two papers which I have received from Mr. Wellesley, the one being the extract of an affidavit sworn by Dr. B—— referring to a letter to Dr. B—— from Mr. H——, who is, I understand, your Law agent; and the other the report of a speech by Mr. S——, who is counsel for the late Mrs. Wellesley's family in the case now under discussion in the Court of Chancery.

" In both it is represented that the whole family on both sides, including myself, *are desirous the children should remain as they are*, and *deprecate the children falling into his hands*, meaning Mr. Wellesley's hands.

" I beg leave to refer you to the two letters which I wrote in the end of November and beginning of December last, in both of which, as well as in the conversation which I had the honour of having with you, I particularly desired to be understood as disclaiming any knowledge of the transactions which led to the suit in Chancery, and as desiring to have nothing to say to the discussion which had taken place or which might take place thereafter upon the question of guardian or no guardian to the children.

" My reason for making this stipulation was obvious, and referred principally to the welfare of the children themselves, and I confess that I am much surprised that after this communication had thus been formally made to you, your Law agent should on the 27th of November, 1826, have allowed Dr. B—— to refer to a letter written in October, 1825, upon which I will observe presently; and should have instructed Mr. S—— to say what he did on the 11th of April, 1826.

" When Mr. H—— wrote on the 17th October, 1825, he must have presumed to write that as fact of which he must have been ignorant, at least as far as

what he wrote related to me ; but when he allowed
Dr. B—— to refer in his affidavit of February,
1826, to his letter of October, 1825, he must have
acted without reference to you ; or if he referred to
you he must have forgotten your instructions, as
you would not have failed to inform him that not
only I had never so expressed myself as is stated in
his letter of October, 1825, but that on the contrary
I had especially stipulated that on the question of
guardian or no guardian I was to have nothing to
say.

"It is with the utmost regret that I trouble you
upon the subject ; but I earnestly entreat you, for the
sake of my veracity and consistency, and for the
sake of your sister's children, if you still wish that I
should eventually have anything to do with the
charge of them, to direct your agents and counsel to
take the earliest opportunity of contradicting as far
as they regard me the assertions made in Mr.
H——'s letter of 1825 and in Mr. S——'s speech of
April, 1826.

> "Ever, my dear Madam,
> "Yours most faithfully,
> "WELLINGTON."

The Duke having received a satisfactory explana-
tion, Miss Long received the following letters from
him :—

"*London,*
"*May* 30*th*, 1826.

"My dear Madam,—Since I wrote to you yesterday I have had reason to believe that Lord Maryborough had already communicated with Mr. S—— on the subject on which I wrote to you.

"I think therefore, upon the whole, and particularly as I have had no communication with Lord Maryborough, and am so unwilling to talk to him upon a subject so distressing to him, that it would be best that Mr. H—— should instruct Mr. S—— in conformity with the suggestion in the first part of my letter of yesterday, and in regard to myself alone.

"Ever, my dear Madam,

"Yours most faithfully,

"WELLINGTON."

"*London,*
"*February* 8*th*, 1827.

"My dear Madam,—I received your letter on my return to town yesterday, and I am very sorry that I did not know you were at Brighton when I was there, as I should have waited upon you.

"Nothing has occurred to prevent me from undertaking the charge which I had engaged to undertake when I last communicated with you upon the subject, and you are fully authorized to name me as one of the guardians of your nephews and niece on the

conditions stated in the first letters which I wrote
you upon this subject.

"I have reason to believe that Mr. Wellesley
intends to appeal from the late decision in Chancery,
which is the reason for my still wishing that the
conditions should be adhered to.

"Ever, my dear Madam,

"Yours most faithfully,

"WELLINGTON."

"*London,*

"*July* 10*th*, 1827.

"Dear Madam,—I have received your note, and
I entirely concur in opinion with you and your sister
that it is desirable that no more time should be lost
in sending your nephews to Eton.

"They might go under charge of Mr. Pitman;
and board at a dame's house with him. They must,
besides, have a school tutor.

"I will take the first opportunity of calling upon
you, and state anything further which may be
necessary.

"Ever, dear Madam,

"Your most faithful Servant,

"WELLINGTON."

"*Apethorpe,*

"*October* 15*th*, 1827.

"Dear Madam,—I have received the enclosed

letter from Mr. Wagner, which it may be desirable
to give to your sister to see.

"I think it proper to tell you that there is a Mr.
Wright, a Fellow of Eton College, who is, I believe,
a brother of an agent of Mr. Long Wellesley's, and
connected with the person to whom he intended to
entrust the education of his daughter.

"I recommend you to give notice that the boys
should have leave to go to nobody even to dinner,
excepting accompanied by their tutor, Mr. Pitman.

"Yours most faithfully,

"WELLINGTON."

"*Sudbourne Hall,*

"*October 25th,* 1827.

"Dear Madam,—I have received your letter of
the 22nd inst., and I have likewise received from
Mr. Nixon the copy of the letter which Mr. Pitman
had written to you on the 20th inst.

"If I am not mistaken, the Master in Chancery
had entertained a discussion, and had even doubted
whether Mr. Pitman ought to be sent to Eton with
your nephews; Mr. Pitman, whom their mother had
placed about them, who had had charge of their
education from their childhood, and of whom the
late Chancellor had approved.

"This being the case, it may well be doubted
whether if Mr. Pitman retires the Master will allow

you to put about your nephews another private
tutor; more particularly as it is quite certain that
Mr. Wellesley will object to anybody selected
by you.

"I would recommend to you, then, first to
endeavour to prevail upon Mr. Pitman to remain, if
not till the Christmas vacation, at least till you can
ascertain whether the Master will allow you to get
another tutor.

"I would then recommend to you to proceed,
under the advice of your counsel, to ascertain
whether it is necessary to consult the Master in
Chancery before you employ another tutor. If it is
not, I will immediately enquire for and recommend
one to you. If it is, you must ascertain from your
counsel whether it is advisable that you should have
the tutor before you go before the Master or afterwards, and I will act accordingly. But the first
point of all is to prevail upon Mr. Pitman, and to
give you time to make these enquiries and arrangements.

"Ever, dear Madam,
"Yours faithfully,
"WELLINGTON."

Miss Long then consulted the Duke as to the
choice of tutors for the boys, and sent him this ex-
planatory note:—

" Binfield Manor, near Bracknell,
" October 26th, 1827.

" I take the liberty of troubling your Grace with one more note, in addition to the one my sister wrote on Sunday, just to explain that we do not ask your Grace's advice, on the subject of naming a tutor for our nephews, in order to quote you as our authority, but merely for our private information and guidance as to whom we should propose to the Master in Chancery or the Court as a substitute. Mr. Hutchinson, whom we have consulted, advised us to adopt this course.   Should your Grace not happen to know of any fit person for the office, I believe the heads of colleges at Oxford are sometimes consulted on these points, and even the bishops.

" I have the honour to be,
" Your Grace's obliged and faithful servant,
" (Signed) D. TYLNEY LONG.
" Duke of Wellington."

The Duke fully entered into the matter, and the following letters concerning it were written by him to Miss Long :—

" Sudbourne Hall,
" October 26th, 1827.

" Dear Madam,—I have received your letter, and I have made enquiries respecting a tutor for your nephews, the result of which I will inform you of.

"Ever yours most faithfully,

"WELLINGTON."

"*S. Saye,*

"*November* 17*th*, 1827.

"Dear Madam,—I have received your letter of the 15th inst., and I have again written to Mr. Wagner respecting the gentleman whom he recommended as the tutor of your nephews.

"Of course you will let Mr. Hutchinson know all that Mr. Wellesley may have done or may do regarding your nephews.

"I was afraid that something of the kind that has occurred would be the consequence of the separation from them of Mr. Pitman.

"Ever, dear Madam,

"Yours most faithfully,

"WELLINGTON."

Mr. Long Wellesley having visited his sons at Eton, Miss Long wrote an account of his having seen them to the Duke, as she feared seeing their father might have unsettled their minds. The Duke replied as follows :—

"*Strathfieldsaye,*

"*November* 20*th*, 1827.

"Dear Madam,—I have received your note, and I

confess I expected that the consequences which you have announced would follow Mr. Wellesley's visit to his sons.

" I hope soon to be able to recommend a tutor. I hope the advice given to his sons, and the sense Dr. Keate entertains of it, will be in evidence.

" Ever yours most faithfully,

" WELLINGTON."

" *London,*

" *January 9th,* 1828.

" My dear Madam,—I enclose you further letters regarding Mr. Campbell ; and I beg you to consider as confidential what Mr. Wagner says respecting that gentleman and Mr. Leason.

" I believe Mr. Leason would be the best, upon the whole.

" I earnestly recommend that you should not send back the boys to Eton without a private tutor.

" Ever yours most faithfully,

" WELLINGTON."

The boys were, therefore, placed under the guardianship of the Duke of Wellington, their father's uncle, and Mr. Windsor, their mother's uncle, and frequent accounts of them are found in letters from the Duchess to the Misses Long.

It is interesting to note how the Iron Duke—the hero of Waterloo—the most prominent figure at the

coronation of George the Fourth, so tenderly undertook, and so carefully performed, the private duty,
which devolved upon him, as guardian to his great-
nephews and niece.

The daughter, the child whom her mother had
called her little angel, became the special charge of
her maternal aunts. Faithfully and devotedly did
the Misses Long fulfil their sacred trust. Sir George
Dallas thus wrote to Miss Long, about three years
after their sister's death :—

" Happy indeed, at last, was your dear departed
sister, when called from her interesting and deserted
children, to the reward of her virtues, to feel, in her
last moments, that she left behind her a fostering
wing that would shelter them with a kindred
maternal care, and well indeed have you both
discharged the anxious duty her cruel fate and
premature death bequeathed to you both. I trust
your dear little niece is quite well, and improving
every way to your satisfaction."

In another letter, this same friend of the family
wrote : " Your sister and you, whatever may be the
result, will have nobly done your duty to these
precious, but unfortunate children."

Once a year the young Victoria was taken to
Apsley House, where, under the care of the Duchess
of Wellington, her father was permitted to see her.
He also occasionally visited his boys at Eton.

The little Victoria certainly charmed her great-aunt, the Duchess of Wellington, who wrote this pleasing opinion of her when she was eleven years old :—

" *Strathfieldsaye,*
" *September* 22*nd*, 1829.

" My dear Miss Long,—I received your kind letter of the 19th this morning, and thank you for it a thousand times. I rejoice to hear that your dear little niece, Victoria, is well again ; will you give her my love and kind remembrance ?

" You do me justice, my dear Miss Long, in being convinced that the real welfare of the children, for whom you are so deeply interested, will be my first object, and I do hope to fulfil the duties of guardian as you, and all those interested for the happiness of the children, would wish them to be fulfilled.

" I never in my life saw a more engaging child than this dear little Victoria ! Docile, sweet-tempered, cheerful and affectionate, while her information appears to me, far to exceed what could be expected from her youth, yet she never appeared fatigued, either with her studies or with her occupations ; she is, indeed, a lovely little girl. Her brothers I never saw but once, and then they were children in frocks.

" I am glad you like your new residence. With your enjoyment of the country, your discernment of its real beauties, I think it likely that you draw, is that the case? if so, being placed in a picturesque situation affords double enjoyment.

" I think my cold is gone.

" God help you, my dear Miss Long. Pray remember me most kindly to your sister.

" And believe me,

" Most truly yours,

" D. C. WELLINGTON."

From the time when the boys were sent to school, Miss Long seems to have had the principal care of them. The choice of tutors, and the arrangements for their holidays, always devolved upon her and her sister. In all little difficulties and all accounts of their childish illnesses, the tutors referred to the Misses Long. The little Victoria became to them as a daughter. Their maternal care of her was rewarded by the sweetness of her disposition, the love she ever manifested towards them, and the diligence with which she pursued her studies. From all that is written or said of her, a pleasanter, or more engaging child could hardly have been found. Her childhood was, of necessity, a very solitary one, and the care taken of her was very strict and vigilant. But in being the centre of so much love, there was also much to make her life happy. The goodness of her disposition was shown by her great attachment

to her governesses. Two of them, Miss Deacon and
Mademoiselle de Joux were her special favourites,
and when she grew up she showed them kindness
and affection to the last days of their lives. Although
Victoria Long Wellesley did not often see her
brothers, she was, in her childhood and afterwards,
on the most affectionate terms with them.

When James Long Wellesley was a little fellow at
Eton, he suffered from an illness brought on from a
somewhat ridiculous cause. At that time, it was
the custom for the man who made birch rods for the
use of the school to sit in a hedge, where he pursued his unpopular occupation. The boys, (James
Wellesley among the number), were in the habit of
teasing and worrying this man over his work. One
day, being more than usually provoked, he seized a
broom which lay near at hand, and belaboured the
boys who attacked him. As he dealt his blows right
and left, James Wellesley came in for a very severe one
on the back of his neck. The next day the poor boy
was taken sick and ill. Consequently he was laid up
for a short time. An account of this occurrence was
duly sent to Miss Long by his tutor, Mr. Dawson.
His sister Victoria then wrote a letter to her brother,
which is alluded to by Mr. Dawson in the following
terms, in again writing to Miss Long : " I believe
his sister's letter did him as much good as anything,
for it actually delighted him, and had all the effect of

UNSTED WOOD, GODALMING.

(From a pencil sketch by DAVID COX.*)*

the best possible restorative. I shall begin to fancy
that she is a little fairy, and that she has positively
bewitched her brother, so that if he is ill again I
shall try for another charm from her to cure him."
In another letter Mr. Dawson thus wrote : " I think
I may assure Miss Long Wellesley that her letter
was received by her brother James with the greatest
delight, and that he means to answer it very soon.
It is very pleasing and instructive to me to observe
how constantly she is in his thoughts, and how
remarkably fond he seems to be of her. The truth
is, he is a boy of exquisite sensibility."

The Misses Long were, at that time, residing at a
pretty place they had rented near Godalming. It
was called Unsted Wood.[1] Here the young Victoria
passed the days of her childhood and early youth.

In the seclusion of that quiet home, and under
the tender care of her noble-minded aunts, the child
pursued her studies and improved under their supervision. With her bright face and cheerful temper,
she must have been like a sunbeam in their home.

The Misses Long were self-denying almost to
austerity, and they brought up their niece on the
strict and old-fashioned lines now so little adhered to.

She once related how, when her governess was at
Sunday evening Church, she was privileged to sit

[1] The picture of Unsted Wood is taken from a pencil sketch by
David Cox.

E

with her aunts during their late dinner. She was then allowed to take some potatoes and gravy. "And," she added, "I used to wish for meat, but I never got it."

In her very early years her brothers sometimes spent their holidays with their aunts, and sometimes were sent, with their tutor, to spend them at Seagry House on the Draycot estate. As time went on Victoria Wellesley saw less and less of these much-loved brothers ; for, unfortunately, their father managed, later on, to get the custody of his sons, and his influence over them was not for good.

At Unsted Wood, in the quiet retirement of the country, Mrs. Long Wellesley's little daughter passed her life quietly and peacefully until she was twelve years old, and then a strange and unlooked-for event occurred, which might have materially altered the course of her future life. On a summer's afternoon in July the Misses Long went for their usual drive, leaving their little niece under the care of her governess at home. On returning from their drive they met a carriage driving away from Unsted. To their amazement they saw in it Mr. Long Wellesley and his eldest son. Seated between them in that carriage was their beloved niece Victoria, looking in the greatest possible distress and misery. It was of no use to try to stop the carriage, or to attempt any parley with the determined father, who felt he had a right to take away his own daughter. So the distressed and frightened ladies drove home. When they reached Unsted Wood they found that Mr. Long Wellesley, attended by four men armed with pistols, had surrounded the house at about six o'clock. The servants had made what resistance they could, but to no avail. The father succeeded in capturing and carrying off his child. Mr. Long Wellesley told the servants he had the authority of the Lord Chancellor, but that the Misses Long could not believe, especially as he showed no written authority.

The Misses Long were, of course, in a most disturbed state of mind. In half an hour, however, they were so far able to collect their thoughts as to write, and at once despatch an account of the proceeding to a trusted friend of the family, Mr. Courtney, imploring his assistance.

From July 15th to the end of August the little girl was under the care of her father. Her aunts spent that period in making every effort in their power to recover her. Six weeks, however, passed away, and the end of August still found them in intense anxiety about their darling charge. At last, in September, some hope of receiving her back seems to have dawned. For, as if something had to do with her own choice, Mr. Courtney, on the 3rd of September, wrote a letter of grave advice to the child, warning her that if she remained where she was, her future life and prospects would be damaged; but, that if she returned to her highly respected aunts, everyone would think well of her. He begged her to let no present enjoyment of any childish pleasure given to her, interfere with the duty of returning to the aunts who had so well cared for her. It was a painful letter for a girl of twelve to receive, and her sensitive mind must have much suffered at the thought that her father, towards whom she owed filial love, notwithstanding all, was not to have the care of her. The letter from Mr. Courtney, however, seems to have been very successful; for, a few days later, Mr. Bulkely, the lawyer, succeeded in gaining possession of her, and took her first to Paris and thence on to England.

Mr. Courtney wrote to Miss Long, speaking well of the little girl's behaviour, and saying he hoped she would soon receive her back.

The darling child, whom the Misses Long fondly called "our dear little wanderer," must have returned to them before the 8th of September in that year, for a letter to Miss Long from Mr. Courtney of that date, expresses the hope that she had by this time been brought back to Unsted Wood. Not only did she return to her aunts safe and well, but unchanged in herself.

It is probable that no one but the aunts, who possessed the confidence of this precious child, ever heard what took place during the period when she was with her father abroad. Perhaps even the Misses Long did not question her, and were ready to respect the conflicting feelings through which she must have passed.

But the satisfaction the Misses Long felt in the niece, now doubly dear to them after this brief separation, is reflected in these words of Sir George Dallas, in reply to some account of her which must have been sent to him by Miss Long: "I derived great pleasure from your most welcome letter of the 12th, conveying to me the glad tidings of the recovery of your niece, and of the final decision of the Chancellor that she should remain with your sister and yourself. The account you gave me in that letter of the state of her mind and feelings on returning to yourselves, was highly interesting, and shows her heart to be naturally so well disposed that it warranted the conclusion that she will, when her education is finished, 'put forth good fruit in due season,' and become an honour to her family and a source of happiness to yourselves. I hear she is every way improved, and your relation, Lady Devonshire, tells me she heard an excellent account of her lately from the Dowager Lady D——." He then speaks of her as pursuing steadily those studies which eventually are calculated to insure her temporal and eternal happiness. Sir George Dallas' words seem now like a prophecy, for no one could more have fulfilled what he hoped she would be than this young girl, who was afterwards destined to be the last of her race.

Her mother called her an angel in her infancy. She merited that title to the last hour of her life.

When she was thirteen she lost her great-aunt, the Duchess of Wellington. The loss is alluded to by her brother James in one of his letters: " I suppose you have heard of the melancholy termination of all the poor Duchess's sufferings ? She died on Saturday morning. She has borne her sufferings with resignation and cheerfulness. Her loss will be felt by everybody who knew her, and particularly by you, to whom she was so kind."

CHAPTER VI.

Fresh Scenes.

AT a very early age Miss Long Wellesley made it her endeavour to do good and to show kindness to all with whom she had to do. When she was only sixteen she wrote many kind letters to a former servant of her aunts, who afterwards became housekeeper to the Duke and Duchess of Gloucester at Bagshot Park. These letters were gratefully acknowledged, and in 1834 this account of the death of the Royal Duke[1] was sent to Miss Long Wellesley in return for the sympathy she had shown for the sad event.

> "*Bagshot Park,*
> "*December 9th,* 1834.

"My dear Miss Long Wellesley,—I had this morning the comfort and consolation of receiving your kind letter; and I beg to assure you of my

[1] Duke of Gloucester, grandson of Frederick Prince of Wales.

grateful sense of the sympathy your aunts and yourself so kindly express for me ; and your solicitude
concerning the amiable and excellent Duchess. Her
Royal Highness[1] supported herself through the whole
of the afflicting scene with astonishing and exemplary
fortitude ; but a frame so weak as that of the Duchess
must naturally sustain a severe shock at an event so
unexpected, but which she endured with perfect
resignation. She is now better; indeed, I may say,
as well as we could have ventured to anticipate
under so severe a trial.

" That personage, whose loss we so deeply and
sincerely lament, was from the first of his being
taken ill, impressed with the idea that he should not
recover; and, on finding himself grow worse, sent
for all his most intimate friends in order to take a
final leave of them.

" He was a truly good man, of eminent piety,
which appeared through his whole conduct, influenced all his actions, and shone most con-
spicuously in his last moments. He received the
sacrament twice during his illness. He said he was
entirely resigned to his fate ; that he had no wish to
return to the world ; informed his chaplain to make
it known that he died in peace with all the world.
His death was the most composed and happy that
can be imagined. He sunk apparently into a com-

---

[1] Princess Mary, daughter of George the Third.

posed sleep, his countenance exhibiting the most tranquil and happy expression. The Duchess, and Princess Sophia Matilda, were constant attendants at his bedside. The Duchess was not suffered to remain with him in his last moments; it was feared the scene would be too much for her; but his sister remained with him till life was extinct. To her the loss is indeed great, and she feels it acutely, but bears it with the fortitude she has evinced from the beginning.

"It gives me great pleasure to know that your aunts and yourself are in the enjoyment of health, to which your frequent change of abode must greatly contribute. This frequent change of scene must be very pleasant and make your time pass very agreeably. I will not forget Mademoiselle de Joux's brother if I should be so fortunate as to hear the situation you mention.

"Pray give my duty to your aunts, and

   "Believe me,

      "My dear Miss Long Wellesley,

         "Your devoted and affectionate Servant,

            "C. M. SCHARSCHMIDT."

When Miss Long Wellesley was seventeen, the Misses Long decided on changing their residence. They then gave up Unsted Wood, and took a place called Ashfold, in Sussex. Their niece felt much natural regret at leaving the place where the greater part of her childhood had been passed.

She thus writes from Ashfold, to her aunts at Unsted Wood : " Notwithstanding all the charms of novelty, my constant heart feels some few pangs at the loss of former delights. I think with painful pleasure of the beautiful common, and all our dear friends the inhabitants thereof."

In another letter, with the sunny cheerfulness of her character, she wrote : " I daresay we shall find beauties which will attach us to Ashfold in like manner as here." For Miss Long Wellesley, under the care of her French governess, Mdlle. de Joux, preceded the Misses Long, and arrived at Ashfold to prepare for their arrival there.

With the practical good sense which always distinguished her, she wrote to her aunts, assuring them that their beds had been well aired, that there had been good fires in every room, and that Bingley and Eliza (two of the maids) would sleep in the bedrooms prepared for them that night. She described the delight of her little dog at seeing her again. She dwelt cheerfully on the beauties of their new residence, though snow lay deep on the ground and rain was falling fast. She looked forward, with affectionate anticipation, to their arrival at Ashfold on the following Wednesday. For her governess, Mdlle. de Joux, Miss Long Wellesley always felt a

very deep attachment. Some time after her education was finished, she took a great deal of trouble to
discover her dear old governess's whereabouts. She
remembered her in many ways. When she had a
house of her own, she invited her to spend a long
visit with her. She also allowed her an annuity to
the end of her life. No one who knew Miss Long
Wellesley could fail to be struck with her bright
disposition, or her care and thought for others. In
her girlhood there seems to have been nothing of the
ordinary thoughtlessness of youth about her. At
the same time she was bright and cheerful, and
often full of fun. She wrote once a letter to her
Aunt Dora, beginning with this couplet :—

> "And I will be so bold,
> Though I'm not very old,
> As to give you a scold
> On your catching a cold."

She then added : "Oh ! how sublime ! I should
never have thought myself such a charming poetess.
Mais revenons a nos moutons. It would be a very
great satisfaction to me if I could be so fortunate as
to effect a slight change in your views of some small
matters of prudence respecting your own dear self.
I fear this poor dear person is often very much
neglected by its owner, who is inclined to think it
of less consequence than those who are residing
with it ! " Then followed certain loving pieces of

advice about Miss Long's health. We hope that
the aunt followed the sage advice of the niece, and
consented to take more care of herself.

The Misses Tylney Long were essentially of the
old school. They held to the opinions in which
they had been brought up. They sat in straight-
backed chairs, and considered footstools superfluous.
They thought fires in bedrooms self-indulgent. They
were courteous, with that studious regard to good
manners in which the high-born people of the last
century excelled. They possessed at that time good
incomes, which had increased by careful economy.
They considered they owed their knowledge of
business and their good management of money a
good deal to the advice of their mother's trustee,
John Barry, who was a great economist and an
excellent financier. The economy, however, which
they exercised themselves was never practised on
others. For they were benevolent and liberal to
the last degree. No tale of distress ever reached
their ears but found from them immediate relief.
They subscribed to many charities. They abounded
in good works. They were ever kind and charitable
to the poor. Two sisters more united than were
the Misses Long could rarely be found. They lived
in closest bonds of love. They did everything
together. They wrote at the same table, enjoyed
the same pursuits, and used the same things. With

such excellent examples before her, it was no wonder that Miss Long Wellesley, with her naturally good disposition, followed in their footsteps of benevolence, and became, in her turn, a blessing to all around her. Miss Long Wellesley paid one, if not more, visits to her guardians, the Duke and Duchess of Wellington, at Strathfieldsaye, from which place several letters are dated to her aunts, expatiating on the pleasures she was enjoying there. When she was eighteen she was duly presented at the Court of King William.

She wrote from London to her aunts, alluding to her approaching presentation. It was a cold day in February, and she hoped the weather would not be quite so winterly when the day fixed for the drawing-room arrived.

The King, who had known her mother and had visited at Wanstead, took special notice of the young *debutante*. When she appeared soon afterwards at one of the Court parties, he said he wished "to watch that little fairy dance."

Miss Long Wellesley's love and gratitude to her aunts was shown in many ways, which must have been very gratifying to their feelings. On one occasion she wrote to her Aunt Dora on receiving some presents :—

"What can I say for such heaps of bountiful goodness? I am confounded with gratitude and admiration, and from the first to the last I cannot

express my thanks in proper, in becoming terms. I
am much annoyed at having nothing to offer in return
for these and all other innumerable and precious
bounties you have ever bestowed on unworthy
little me. I beg most affectionately to respond to
your wishes for our mutual enjoyment of joys and
delights, of which we have but a very small idea
here below. I fervently pray for your entire satisfaction and happiness through the present and all
succeeding years, and that I may not prove myself
totally unworthy of the great blessings I am permitted to enjoy at your liberal hands. I further
pray to be found ever your very grateful and
affectionate niece,

" V. Long Wellesley."

In another letter, dated 1838, she wrote, after
wishing her aunt all happiness in the New Year:
" I trust that I shall not fail to contribute whatever
is in my small power to further these desirable ends.
I hope I need not repeat that such is at all times
my greatest desire, in return for the innumerable
blessings I receive at your bountiful hands."

On another occasion Miss Long Wellesley wrote,
in acknowledgment of presents sent her by her
aunts: " What can I say in return for such a heap
of beautiful presents, accompanied by such loving
and amiable inscriptions. The first thing which

occurs to me is that I am extremely unworthy of the immensity of good you have loaded me with, throughout my poor little life, by your means made happy and comfortable in the greatest degree. My next hope is that, though much surrounded by great and manifold imperfections, I may, by imploring higher aid than my own poor endeavours, never do anything displeasing, or in the slightest degree painful to you."

On another occasion she wrote to her aunt these words : "I am unhappily but too well aware that impatience and dislike of restraint are not such utter strangers to my heart as you seem often to imagine, but still I can most sincerely assure you that when I think I have said or done that which is not pleasing to you, I have a thousand torments for my edification, and, I trust, further improvement."

It was by such loving words as these, and by such efforts to do all that was pleasing to them, that Miss Long Wellesley sought to repay her aunts' kind care of and affection for her.

CHAPTER VII.

The Young Queen.

VERY early in life Miss Long Wellesley manifested the most earnest religious feeling, great moral rectitude, and a strong sense of the responsibilities of life. The pomps and gaieties of the high rank to which she belonged had very little charm for her, and often gave rise to grave reflections. She was staying with friends in London at the time of the Coronation of Queen Victoria. She writes in this thoughtful strain to her aunts on the approaching event: "This leads me to the engrossing subject of the present superabundantly gay and full season, viz., the Coronation of our much beloved and amiable Queen. I do sincerely hope she has some real friend near her, who will lead her mind to consider the important ceremony which is fast approaching, in the light in which our excellent pastor treated it in his two beautiful sermons of last Sunday, and then surely it cannot be regarded as a mere idle pageant; and happy would it be for all the multitudes who will be assembled on this great occasion, if they have the same exalted ideas inspired to them; and this makes me consider how every circumstance in this bustling scene of life may be turned to advantage of the highest nature. I sincerely hope that the poor and miserable, of whom there will necessarily be great numbers in the crowd, will have much of holy and devout feelings inspired to them, and then how much fewer crimes will be committed than are unfortunately general in such seasons." .

Such were the reflections of the girl, who was but one year older than the girl Queen, who has since fulfilled the highest expectations and the most sanguine hopes of the nation she was so early called upon to rule.

Upon going to one of the Court parties held soon after the Queen's marriage, Miss Long Wellesley expresses herself to her aunts as not quite happy because they were not with her, and then goes on to say : " I consider these shows as fine lights and, therefore, pretty things to see now and then. Of course, Prince Albert, being a novelty and a most fascinating bridegroom, added to the interest of the scene. But for all that, I am happy to say, I feel more and more disinclined to place my happiness amongst such glittering and dazzling festivities. I trust I shall never be called upon to be much

F

amongst them. I thought the Queen, as well as
her royal spouse, looked, (though at moments in
good spirits), much oppressed with weighty business. The Queen was in black gauze and silk,
with loads of magnificent diamonds, and certainly
looked extremely well. Prince Albert, in a splendid
Hussar uniform, waltzing charmingly with the
Princess Augusta."

Miss Long Wellesley then gave a list of the friends
she had met, and mentioned that she was presented
to the Duke of Cambridge, who gave Lord Maryborough a very nice account of some of the pictures.
" There was a very magnificent supper, to which the
Queen had just repaired, followed by her loving and
hungry subject, her lowliest slave among the rest,
who devoured some well cut chicken and wine and
water, after which we came home, waiting but a very
short time for the carriage, to which vehicle I was
conducted by Master Charles Somerset."

When Miss Long Wellesley was twenty her aunts
intended taking her to Rome. Her delight at this
projected tour abroad was shown in a cleverly
written French letter, which was passed, as a surprise, through her aunt Dora's bedroom door. It
was, probably, at this time that the Misses Long
gave up their residence at Ashfold. The idea of
going to Rome was, however, set aside. Instead of
this, Miss Long Wellesley was taken by her aunts

for a tour through various parts of England and South
Wales. To the young and untravelled all things
are new. So the young Victoria, entered with
enthusiastic delight, into this her first tour of
pleasure. With the usual cheerfulness of her disposition, she seems to have expressed no disappointment at not going to Rome. The Misses Long and
their niece left London in August and travelled
about until the following April. They drove by
Windsor and Eton, and on to Oxford. From thence
they went to Malvern and Worcester. Miss Long
Wellesley kept a diary of this tour, and duly marked
down in it all they did and all that interested her.
While at Worcester she visited the pottery works.
The house used for these works was, of course, of
great interest to her, as having been the ancient
mansion house of her grandmother's family, the
Earls of Plymouth. From Worcester they journeyed
on into South Wales, staying at Aberystwith and
Tenby. There is a very fresh and healthy tone
about Miss Long Wellesley's diary. Only on one
day did she feel miserable, and that was when she
had seen a boy ill-treating a dog. She then put
down her reflections as to the mysterious dispensa-
tion which allows innocent animals to suffer. She
met with various friends on her travels, and felt
much pleasure in exchanging visits with them.
After a more lengthened stay at Tenby the travellers

went to Leamington. There they remained a little time, and Miss Long Wellesley enjoyed going to a few balls.

They all came back to London in April, to a house in Harley Street. There Miss Long Wellesley ended her diary with the following reflections :—

" Came very nearly to the same spot from whence we set out eight months ago. Many wonderful and interesting sights have we seen in that period, as this little book testifies, which, having been my faithful companion and mirror of all my actions during these our travels, I will now lay aside for the present, hoping all I have seen may not be quite thrown away upon me, and that every day I may grow wiser and better, whether I remain quietly and end my days in one spot, or whether it be my destiny to travel from one end of the world to the other ; and may I now and always put my trust in that Gracious Being Who has till now so wonderfully preserved me through all the events of my little life."

The following year the Misses Long again went with their niece for another tour to Bath, Bristol, and various parts of Somerset and Wilts, staying, as before, for some time at Leamington. In 1842, when Miss Long Wellesley was twenty-two, they settled down with her at Albourne Place, near Hurst-pierpoint, Sussex. There they remained for sixteen years. At Albourne Place Miss Long Wellesley contracted a friendship with Miss Hasker, a young lady some years her junior, whose parents took a country place near. This lady described Miss Long Wellesley as she was at twenty-six, bright, cheerful, and kind-hearted. Her eyes were of a rich blue, and she had an abundance of pretty light hair, which she wore in flowing curls round her face in the fashion then prevalent. Those who gained the friendship of Miss Long Wellesley kept it to the end of her life, for she was always constant and faithful in her attachments. In later years, when she had an establishment of her own, Miss Hasker became one of her most welcome guests.

For David Cox (whose pupils her aunts had been) Lady Victoria retained an affectionate remembrance. When a life of this artist came out, she wrote these words in the margin of the book : " Well do I remember the dear old man when he used to stay for a fortnight or more with us; one of my earliest friends, whose memory I shall always cherish with hearty affection, and rejoice to find so true a description of his character and genius in this valuable memoir of his life."

CHAPTER VIII.

Bereavements and Changes.

CONTINUED interest had always been taken in Miss Long Wellesley by her grand-parents, Lord and Lady Maryborough, and by her great-uncle and aunt, the Duke and Duchess of Wellington. Miss Long Wellesley received an affectionate letter from her grandmother, on the engagement of another grand-daughter, in which she said: " I cannot have any doubt but that you will be pleased to hear of any event which gives Lord Maryborough and me satisfaction. I therefore hasten to announce to you the intended marriage of Emily Bagot to Lord Winchelsea. It is in every respect most desirable, and I consider her most fortunate."

Lady Maryborough then expresses affectionate wishes for her grand-daughter Victoria's future. In 1842 Lord Maryborough inherited the Earldom of Mornington, upon the death of his eldest brother, Marquis Wellesley, who left no children. Lord

Mornington only bore the title for three years. He died in 1845, when Miss Long Wellesley was twenty-seven. Her father, then Viscount Wellesley, succeeded him, as the fourth Earl of Mornington. Her eldest brother became Viscount Wellesley, and her second brother the Hon. James Wellesley. Her own title from that date was Lady Victoria Pole Tylney Long Wellesley. "A very long name," she used to say, "for a little person to have."

The death of the grandfather, who had been so kind a father-in-law to her mother, and to whom she was much attached, was naturally a grief to Lady Victoria. These appropriate words were written to her by one of her friends, Miss Anderson: "The great age and long illness of your grandfather must have prepared all his numerous family and relatives for this termination of his trial, but how little can one regret the prolonged suffering of a few weeks, or even months, on this side the grave, when one reflects on the bright prospect beyond it opening to those who have laid up a treasure that cannot fade, eternal in the heavens."

Lady Victoria's cousin, the Hon. Charlotte Somerset, a daughter of Lord Raglan, was staying with their grandmother at the time of Lord Mornington's funeral. In an affectionate letter written by her to Lady Victoria, she gives a favourable account of Lady Mornington's health under her bereavement. Miss Somerset adds : " I enclose you some of our dearest grandfather's hair. Oh! my dear Victoria, what a friend and relative we have lost, but, however, we must not repine, for till within the last few years what good health he enjoyed, and we must be grateful that his mind continued so fresh and young to the last ; but still, such a short time after such a sad event, one cannot help feeling it very much."

Lady Victoria's father, who then became the fourth Earl of Mornington, was much overcome at his father's funeral. Soon afterwards he wrote a letter to his mother, asking to see her. He received her permission, and called upon her twice. The interviews were painful ones to Lady Mornington, but still they afforded her some satisfaction. Her son had evidently suffered, for he was looking quite old and his abundant hair was as white as snow. He was then fifty-seven years old.[1] His two sons had much felt the long separation from their sister, but it had not diminished their affection for each other or for their maternal aunts. In a letter written by Mr. James Wellesley to his sister, he says :—

" You may easily guess how happy your letter has

---

[1] In 1845 Lord Wellesley wrote to his sister that their father had taken his seat in the House of Lords, and had been very well received. Also that he had been well received by the Duke of Wellington and the rest of the family.

made me. Believe me, my own dearest sister, that nothing will make me so happy as being again, as soon as I can, on the same terms with you and my aunts that I was when I was a child. God bless you, my dearest sister, and

" Believe me,

" Your very affectionate brother,

" JAMES LONG WELLESLEY."

The Hon. James Wellesley was then in the army, and wrote to his sister from Carlow, where his regiment was quartered. In 1850 his health was in a failing condition. In 1851 he died at Geneva, when he was only thirty-six years old. His death was a great sorrow to his affectionate sister. He was buried at Geneva. Shortly afterwards a cross over his grave was erected to his memory by his only sister, with this inscription :—

SACRED TO THE MEMORY OF

THE HONOURABLE JAMES HENRY FITZROY POLE TYLNEY LONG WELLESLEY,

Second Son of William, Fourth Earl of Mornington, by his Wife, Catherine Tylney Long, eldest daughter and heir of Sir James Tylney Long, Bart.
Born at Wanstead House, Essex,
August 12th, 1815. Died
at Geneva, October
31st, 1851.
"Come unto Me, all ye that are weary and heavy laden, and I will give you rest."

With her eldest brother, Viscount Wellesley, Lady Victoria was always on the most affectionate terms. Their correspondence had been of the most friendly kind. Lord Wellesley had a very warm heart, and in many respects must have had points of sympathy with his sister.

The death of his caretaker at Draycot House, in 1851, was a personal distress to him, and he thus wrote of it to his sister: "I am sure you will be sorry to hear that poor dear old Ellery expired on Monday night at ten o'clock. I have just received this melancholy intelligence. Poor old Ellery had had a bad cold for some time, but was not thought to be in any danger."

The greater part of Lord Wellesley's life had been spent abroad, but he occasionally came to England. In 1853 he wrote to his sister from Draycot, hoping to spend the following Christmas with her and their aunts. In this letter he praises his sister for her care in returning him the baskets, in which he had sent her presents of game. He also tells her he has a Scotch shawl as a present for her.

In another letter from Paris, he mentions that their cousin, the Duke of Wellington, had been doing a good deal to Apsley House, and that Strathfield-saye, which he seemed recently to have visited, was the same as ever. In a letter written from the Clarendon, in 1854, Lord Wellesley then described to Lady Victoria another visit to their cousins:

"I have been down to Strathfieldsaye to sport with the Duke and party. We had a most delightful reunion, and I took one day seven grouse and another day six grouse. This is very good, considering that the Duke has only begun to get up grouse from last May. I was delighted to visit the old place again, as it reminded me of former days. The house is much the same, only it has in some parts been done up, which has greatly improved its appearance. I am starting off to Paris to-morrow.

"Wishing you and my aunts a Merry Christmas and a Happy New Year,

"Believe me,

"Your affectionate brother,

"WELLESLEY."

Letters such as these, showing interest in her plans, a care for her health, and asking to hear about her amusements, passed from Lord Wellesley to his sister.

Like most people who have been abroad a good deal, Lord Wellesley found it difficult to settle in England, so the meetings between him and his sister were, of necessity, few and far between, but when in England he lost no opportunity of seeing Lady Victoria and his aunts.

The life led by the Misses Long had been a somewhat secluded one, for they had suffered much under the trials they had so nobly borne. The sorrows and wrongs of their sister had made such a deep impression upon them that not only had they, since her death, laid aside all thoughts of marriage for themselves, but they also dreaded it for their niece. It must not, however, be supposed that Miss Long Wellesley passed through her girlhood without several suitors for her hand.

In 1848 she accepted the addresses of one of her cousins, and became engaged to him. But this engagement only lasted from the November of 1848 to January, 1849; for her aunts and her brother had reasons for supposing that this proposed marriage would not prove conducive to the happiness of one so precious to them. Lady Victoria's own good judgment coincided with the opinions of her relatives, so the engagement was broken off. When Lady Victoria wrote the last painful letter to her betrothed, returning his letters and explaining her reasons, she did so in such a kind and tender manner that her cousin retained his love for her to the last days of his life. When he was on his death-bed, some years afterwards, she sent him a kind message through his sister. He received and responded to it with tears in his eyes.

The kind and affectionate letter which his sister wrote to Lady Victoria after his death shows how greatly Lady Victoria was valued by the family, and how much they had appreciated the delicate and tender feeling she had shown. So partly from the fear of her aunts that she might be thrown away, and partly from other circumstances, Lady Victoria Wellesley was destined never to marry.

For their niece's sake the Misses Long had emerged from the seclusion in which they had lived, and, on her account, entered more into society. At Albourne, especially, and in London, they gave many pleasant parties for Lady Victoria's entertainment. The early retirement in which they had lived, however, and the worries and cares they had encountered had left an effect upon their nerves. After leaving Draycot, they had found it difficult to settle for long in any definite home. Consequently they moved from time to time to different country places. The one object of their solicitude and care was their beloved niece. It is pleasant to read the little notes, breathing so much affectionate feeling, and entering so fully into all her interests. The coming up of a flower Victoria had planted, (as Miss Long expressed it), "with her own fair hands," was an event worth recording, when on one of her visits from home. They delighted in making her presents, and sometimes some witty words would accompany their gifts. On presenting her with a pair of the long gold earrings then in fashion, Miss Emma Long wrote to Lady Victoria on her birthday: "Many happy years to you, my dear Victoria, but not as long ears as the earrings I have now the pleasure of laying at your feet."

On another of her birthdays Miss Emma Long wrote more solemnly, somewhat anticipating that lot which she and her sister half feared for their beloved charge. These were her words: "A bride and a happy one, I doubt not, you are destined one day to become. You will do me the favour to accept the little serpent brooch, an emblem, as you know, of that eternity to which we are all hastening, and may we all have grace to choose the right path which leads to eternal life. This blessed hope is, indeed, the sovereign balm under all the sorrows and trials of our mortal state."

Lady Victoria's filial love for the beloved aunts who had brought her up, continued not only when she was grown up, but to the end of their lives.

This note, which she wrote to them in 1850, shows her great and unchanging appreciation of their goodness:—

" My dear Aunt,—It is with renewed feelings of gratitude for all the very great blessings I enjoy that I offer you my most fervent wishes that you may see many many more years of enjoyment; brightening the lot of the unfortunate, and shedding happiness, to the utmost of your power, around the path of all you have any connection with. When I consider the various *escapes* of the past year, I cannot but feel doubly grateful that I am still permitted, by a gracious Providence, to be an inmate of so happy a home as mine is, and trusting in future to be preserved from my many follies and shortcomings.

"I ever remain,

" Your most affectionate and devoted niece,

"V. LONG WELLESLEY."

What the faults and shortcomings of so exemplary a character were could not be determined by anyone who knew her. Her judgment of herself reminds one of the words of the hymn—

> "And they who fain would serve Thee best
> Are conscious most of wrong within."

The following pretty sentence is found in a letter to her aunts on New Year's Eve, 1851. She regrets she cannot transcribe some eulogistic and grateful lines to them, and then goes on to say : "I must beg you to accept the will for the deed, and to believe how ardent are the prayers of your child for the very long continued lives of those so precious to many, but to her above all value, as having always been, and to this moment being, the increasing means of the many, very many undeserved blessings she enjoys."

During Lady Victoria Wellesley's residence at Albourne Place, she was laid up with a very serious illness. For a short time her life was in danger. Mr. Weeks, the family doctor, watched over her with the greatest anxiety. When, at last, the crisis was past, he was so overcome that he shed tears of thankfulness. So much was this sweet and tender young life valued and loved by all who came in contact with her. Although she was safely brought through this danger, and happily recovered her health, she felt the effects of her illness for many years.

In the July of 1857 Lady Victoria's father, the Earl of Mornington, died. Little as his daughter had seen of him, his death was a great sorrow to her. Her filial feelings towards her father, combined with her deep sense of her mother's wrongs, formed one of the finest points of her character. Her letters [1] to him were always full of respect and duty. In one of these she wrote that she should "ever pray for his temporal and spiritual welfare." Her manner of bringing in these little touches of feeling was so gentle, that we may hope it tended to help and comfort one who, in his last years, must have been a very lonely man. The news of his

[1] Many affectionate letters were exchanged from time to time between him and his daughter, with whose dutiful feelings towards himself he was always well pleased. He always delighted in seeing her.

death was brought to Lady Victoria Wellesley and the Misses Long at their town house in Portland Place.

The sad event occurred at a time when a party had been arranged for Lady Victoria's special entertainment. The invited guests had, of course, to be put off, and, instead, the mourning dresses were ordered. Madame Batifort, a Court dressmaker, who in several misfortunes had received much kindness from the family, made the mourning for Lady Victoria, who was weeping through the whole time that she was fitted.

Who can tell but that the prayers of this dutiful daughter were answered at the Throne of Grace?

G

CHAPTER IX.

Brother and Sister.

UPON the death of the fourth Earl of Mornington, his eldest and only surviving son,
Viscount Wellesley, succeeded his father
as the fifth Earl. He also, of course, inherited what
might be termed the wreck of his mother's estates
of Draycot, Seagry, Wanstead, Tylney, and other
lands. All this property had been deeply mortgaged,
and, unfortunately, Viscount Wellesley, when he
became of age, had been induced by his father to
cut off the entail. It therefore became his absolutely, with power to will it as he chose. As
Viscount Wellesley was unmarried, and as his only
brother, the Hon. James Wellesley, died unmarried,
Lady Victoria Long Wellesley, like her ancestress,
Lady Emma Child, and her mother, Miss Tylney
Long, became her only brother's heiress presumptive.
But to make "assurance doubly sure," Lord Wellesley, when he became Earl of Mornington, made a
will, in which he bequeathed all the estates which

he had inherited from his mother, to his only sister,
Lady Victoria. Later on he made another will to
the same purport, adding to the former bequest,
various things at his personal disposal he wished his
sister to have. As, however, Lady Victoria was
only three years younger than her brother, and as

THE LAST EARL OF MORNINGTON.

there was the possibility of his marrying, her
position, of course, was a very contingent one.
Upon her father's death Lady Victoria came into
the sum of £13,542. This fortune, though small for
her rank, and smaller still as compared to her
mother's wealth, yet, with what she possessed previously, placed her in an independent position. She

had also arrived at an age when she could, with propriety, start an establishment of her own.

She began by taking a small house at Eastbourne, the air of which peculiarly suited her health. A little time before this the Misses Long had given up their residence at Albourne, and removed to a country place about ten miles distant from it, Bolney Lodge, near Cuckfield. There Lady Victoria usually spent Christmas, and part of the summer, with her aunts, and also went with them, for the London season, to their house in Portland Place. She spent the spring and the autumn at her own little house at Eastbourne, and derived much benefit from its bracing air.

Just at the time when she wanted to secure the services of a really trustworthy servant, she was fortunate enough to hear that a former servant of her mother's, Henry Bicknell, was seeking a situation. The history of this man was much to his credit. He had entered the service of Mr. and Mrs. Long Wellesley at the time of their marriage. He was then only thirteen. He was employed at Wanstead House as steward's room boy. In course of time he worked his way up, and was eventually promoted to be butler and house steward. He had seen and known a good deal of Mrs. Long Wellesley's sorrows. He had known Lady Victoria and her brother from their birth. After Mrs. Long

Wellesley's death he entered the service of the Misses Tylney Long, and remained with them for eight years. He then became house steward to the Duke of Leeds. After the Duke died, he became servant to Colonel Wyndham, at Petworth House, Sussex.

The family had always felt great interest in Bicknell. Soon after Mrs. Long Wellesley's death Miss Long tried, through the Duke of Wellington, to obtain for him some position of trust. To this request the Duke gave this cautious reply :—

" London,
" June 23rd, 1828.

" My dear Madam,—I have received your note, and I should really be very happy to forward your views, but there are at present no vacancies in the office of lending waiter, to which you refer.

" I would besides beg to observe you that Bicknell is, I believe, one of the witnesses in the Wellesley suit in Chancery ; and as it is desirable to prevent further misrepresentations upon that subject, it would be advisable not to appoint him to an office, at least till that cause should be terminated.

" Ever, dear Madam,
" Yours most faithfully,
" WELLINGTON."

With that faith in an over-ruling Providence which Lady Victoria Wellesley so peculiarly held, she regarded it as a special instance of God's care of His servants, that at the very time that Bicknell was out of place and in some distress, she should be requiring a confidential man-servant. She, accordingly, engaged him as butler for her tiny home at Eastbourne, and his wife also entered her service as cook-housekeeper. It was a step she never regretted. Two more affectionate and trustworthy servants could not have existed. They cared for herself and her interests, and served her faithfully to the last days of their life. For Bicknell had a staunch attachment for the old family, and Lady Victoria was delighted to have in her household one who had served her mother. She was proud of the care he took of her. "He takes as much care of me as if I were his daughter," she would sometimes say. She was always pleased and amused at his little acts of almost tyrannical solicitude for her. When she was starting on a journey he would have her boxes brought down three or four hours beforehand, in order that she might be in time. He would light the chamber candles full early, as a hint that it was time her ladyship should retire for the night. She would take a mischievous pleasure in blowing them out when his back was turned. Her first house at Eastbourne was in South Terrace. It was semi-detached. Next door lived the owner of both the houses. This old lady would only let on two conditions—first, that there should be no piano ; second, that no dog should be kept. Now, as Lady Victoria was specially musical, and as she was very fond of little dogs, these two conditions must have involved some amount of self-denial. But Lady Victoria accepted and kept to them with her usual cheerful manner of " making the best of things." While at Eastbourne she took great interest in her poorer neighbours, as she had always done in other places. She took a district, and visited personally, disregarding the advice of her landlady " that her ladyship ought not to go into such dirty houses." She founded a Lending Library for the poor, established it on excellent rules, and kept it under her own supervision. During her residence at Eastbourne her brother, Lord Mornington, who had been away a longer time than usual, returned to England, to her great delight. As they were always on the most affectionate terms, it was a real interest to her to see more of him, to meet him in London, and accompany him to the parties given by their different friends. She treasured up every little instance of his love and care for her. It was always a great pleasure to her to receive him at her little seaside home.

It was Lord Mornington's great desire to receive his aunts and sister at Draycot. The Misses Long

felt some natural reluctance at revisiting the home
of their youth, fraught, as its memories were, with
so much that was happy and painful. At last, however, they consented to accompany their niece for a
week's stay at Draycot House. Very happy was
Lady Victoria at the prospect of seeing again this
cherished place, and of being her brother's guest
there. It was in the late autumn that she and her
aunts took the journey to the old ancestral home.
Lady Victoria ordered several pretty dresses, and
entered, with zest, into the preparations for the visit.
Somewhere between Chippenham and Draycot a
number of the tenants met them. They approached to
take the horses out and draw the carriage themselves
to Draycot House, but the Misses Long felt nervous
at this, so the tenants, with some disappointment,
had to give up the idea. Very warm was the recep-
tion of the three ladies at Draycot. Universal
pleasure was felt by all who saw them, and
they passed a most happy week there. They
also paid another visit to Lord Mornington in
summer weather. Very sweet Lady Victoria looked
on this occasion, as she was seen walking on the
lawn in front of Draycot House. She wore one
of the bright blue silk dresses then so much in
fashion, and the colour reflected itself in the rich
blue of her eyes.

At this time Lady Victoria, notwithstanding

Believe me
always very affte
Godmother

Louy Loddesley

the troubles of her early life, seemed a very happy woman. Her religion was of an essentially cheerful kind. She believed in joy as a fruit of the Holy Spirit. She was ever anxious to influence others for good. She lost no opportunity of doing kindness, great and small. She delighted in preparing little surprises for those she loved. She would receive, with unfeigned pleasure, any present, or any little attention shown to herself. Her nature was open and candid, and she especially admired candour and honesty in others. She was a great reader of character, and possessed wonderful powers of discernment. At the same time, when she detected faults and mistakes in others, she met them with that charity "which never faileth." Her standard of right and wrong was a very high one. She was trustful and affectionate to the last degree. But when once she detected any positive wrong-doing in those with whom she had to do, she would meet it with righteous severity. Her countenance was a very speaking one. It seemed, sometimes, almost transparent, as if the feelings within were reflected in it. Her expression was changing, sometimes clouded with an expression of gravity, at others sparkling with pleasure. Her voice was a cheery one, and her pretty ringing laugh had a very happy sound. She had a great objection to anything that was ultra melancholy or morbid. For the tone of her own mind was essentially healthy. Her manner was a very finished one, and she possessed almost the royal power of putting people at their ease. She exercised, to perfection, the courtesy which peculiarly belongs to the well born, and which, with her, was also the outcome of a loving heart. She may be said to have combined the inherent goodness of the Longs with the fascinating power of the Wellesleys. She was also pre-eminently practical. She was an excellent manager of money, and had the rare art of making it go a long way. She was also liberal with what she possessed, and extremely hospitable. She had a keen appreciation of wit, and was very fond of a joke. The smallest pleasantry would often cause her much amusement. This gentle woman, who was destined never to have a husband's care, ever showed that deep respect and reverence for all superior and worthy men which forms one of woman's greatest charms. She, who was never to fold a child of her own in her arms, had such a motherly heart that she attracted all children to her. As Lady Victoria stood on the Draycot lawn on that summer day, she little thought of what trouble would, ere long, be in store for her. For Lord Mornington was then in good health, and she might fairly have looked forward to many happy visits to Draycot Cerne, and much pleasant intercourse with the brother she loved so well.

CHAPTER X.

Passing Away.

BEFORE Lady Victoria had the opportunity of visiting Draycot again, Lord Mornington's health became a matter of serious anxiety to his relatives. During his residence in Paris, in the spring of 1863, the painful disease, which afterwards proved fatal, began to develop itself.

On the 31st of March, Lady Victoria wrote to her aunts a letter full of apprehension at the accounts she had received. There was some idea of Lord Mornington's coming to England in June, but his sister feared he would not be able to take the journey. She therefore wrote and offered to go to him. For more than a month Lady Victoria remained at Eastbourne, in a state of anxiety and suspense, longing to go to Paris to be with her brother, but not liking to do so until he had decidedly consented to her going. For at that time he did not know, or wished not to consider, that he was in a precarious condition, and believed he might be able to be in London in June.

In the end of April she wrote to her aunts : " I have just received the enclosed, which I think a very bad account, and it makes me anxious for us to be together." After arranging to come to her aunts for a little while, she adds : " There is a beautiful chapter in my little book of Dean Goulbourn, in which he brings forcibly home to me that all events, great and small, are pre-ordained for each individual. Our duty is to make the use of them our Heavenly Father intends we should. The more one advances in life the more one sees the wisdom of leaving all to Him, at the same time that we endeavour to do His will and not our own."

Soon after joining her aunts in London Lady Victoria started for the Continent, escorted by the family doctor, Mr. Weeks, and attended by her faithful maid, Mary Horne, and a courier named Willoy, a Swiss, whom she found a great comfort and help throughout her sojourn abroad. Having arrived at Paris, she went to the Hotel Bristol in the Place Vendôme, which is very near to the Hotel du Rhin, where Lord Mornington was staying.

The Earl of Cowley, her father's first cousin, was at that time H.M. Ambassador at Paris. Thankful to think that she had relatives near her in a strange land, Lady Victoria placed herself under Lord

Cowley's protection. She found her brother in a very weak condition, and suffering much pain. Of his recovery there seemed no hope. Lady Victoria, therefore, made up her mind to remain near him as long as his fast-closing life should last.

Lord Mornington was very glad to see his sister, and arranged that she should visit him every day from two to three o'clock.

Finding her apartments too large and very expensive, Lady Victoria sent out her courier, whom she described as " all activity," to find more economical quarters. He soon succeeded in securing some at the Hotel Mirabeau, which is pleasantly situated in the Rue de la Paix, near the Tuilleries Gardens.

On May 13th she wrote to her aunts, praising the air of Paris, which she describes as very much like Eastbourne, and goes on to say :—

" Our beloved invalid varies very much. Yesterday I was very unhappy about him. He appeared so sadly weak and ill, and evidently thought himself so, but so amiable and thoughtful for myself and others. To-day he is quite another man, talking cheerfully, and, to my great amusement, from telling me I had better go back in a day or two, he proposed I should remove my little establishment from Eastbourne here. He is evidently delighted at my daily visit, which, of course, is a great happiness to me.

" I saw Lady Cowley again to-day. She seems

so good as well as most pleasing and amiable. I
am sorry to say she goes to London for a month
to-morrow, but Lord Cowley remains, and Lord and
Lady Royston are coming, and she hopes I will call
upon them. I have hired a very nice carriage for a
week, an open one, with one horse. The fiacres I
think detestable. Horne and I were taken by our
attentive Willoy round by the Hotel des Invalids,
the Champs de Mars, and up a winding hill where
we had a beautiful view over Paris, and finally found
ourselves in that beautiful Bois de Boulogne, now so
charmingly laid out with lakes, flowering shrubs, etc.,
and we were close to the Emperor, who was walking
at the side of the carriage, with one attendant only,
on whom he leant. He looks dreadfully ill and weak.
He is making extensive and apparently very useful
improvements round Paris. It is really delightful to
have so large a town so utterly free from smoke, the
houses all looking as new and fresh as if they were
only finished yesterday. I hope to go to-morrow to
the Ascension Day Service at the English Chapel
near the Embassy. Lord Cowley told me they
have service in the Embassy every Sunday and
Saint's Day, but very early—half-past nine or a
quarter to ten—only for themselves and any friend
they like to ask. The Embassy is in the Rue St.
Honoré, of course a fine large house with a splendid
garden.

" My poor dear brother used to go to it and sit nearly the whole afternoon."

When Lady Victoria had been a few days in Paris she felt so comfortably situated and so well that she was able to part with her medical attendant, Mr. Weeks. Throughout the month of May she continued her anxious watch over her brother's health. In the frequent letters she wrote to her aunts, she, with her usual cheerfulness, dwelt more on the mercies which surrounded her than on the anxiety which pressed on her spirits. She often compared the air of Paris to that of Eastbourne, and said how well she felt and how wonderfully she was supported. She dwelt much and often on the kindness of Lord Cowley, spoke of a very kind letter she had received from her cousin, the Hon. Gerald Wellesley, then Dean of Windsor, and praised the attention shown to Lord Mornington by his faithful attendant and nurse, Arthur Pallaster. But, most of all, she dwelt on the comfort it was to her to be near her brother. She wished she could do more for him, but felt her daily visit to be a great happiness to both. At first there was some faint hope that Lord Mornington's illness might prove to be a tumour, but very soon this hope was set aside, for it turned out to be cancer in the tongue. This painful disease was fast spreading, and much pain and weakness was undergone by the invalid.

Although he was able to take his daily drives he became weaker and weaker, and his appearance was that of a man bowed down with age. He always enjoyed his sister's visits, and his parting words generally were "come again to-morrow."

In writing to her aunts, Lady Victoria fondly spoke of her brother as " our darling invalid, or our beloved patient," and was never tired of describing his patience through his sufferings, and his consideration for herself and others. The disease was gradually gaining ground, and causing him increased discomfort. He was unable to sleep at night without the aid of chloroform. At last Mr. Dawson told Lady Victoria the painful truth, that the case was a hopeless one, and only a question of time. She was able to keep cheerful when with her brother, but felt on leaving him that her heart would burst. The 29th of May was Lady Victoria's birthday. To her great delight her dear invalid sent her a magnificent bouquet. Her aunts, in writing to her, reminded her that she had never spent a birthday away from them since, on one occasion, in her childhood.

In thanking them for their birthday gift, Lady Victoria affectionately assured her aunts that this fact had been very present to her mind. At times Lady Victoria took interest in the sights of Paris, specially the churches, and felt that such diversions

H

were good for her health and spirits ; but sometimes, and specially on her birthday, her heart turned away from the gay city, which for her and hers had such deeply melancholy recollections. At such times, when she was feeling specially sad, she longed for the quiet enjoyment of her peaceful and happy English home. For Lady Victoria was essentially an Englishwoman in all her associations and feelings, true and loyal from the depth of her heart to her Queen and her country.

However, she always felt that the brief enjoyment of that one daily interview with her only brother more than compensated her for the lonely and anxious hours of the rest of the day, and realized that in after years, it would be one of her greatest consolations to remember she had been so near and seen so much of her beloved and nearest relation in the last days of his life.

The services at the English Church were, of course, a great comfort to her, and she often quoted sentences in the sermons given there which had specially struck her.

At the end of May summer weather was beginning to set in, and Lady Victoria describes her visit to St. Cloud, and how pleasant she had found the shade of the fine old trees. Just then the Emperor was engaged in having the Bois de Boulogne laid out and made into the beautiful pleasure resort it now is, causing, as Lady Victoria expressed it, every other resort to fall into the shade. Lord Mornington then seemed better, and on one day was able to enjoy seeing Lord Cowley and Lady Victoria at the same time. He also derived comfort from the visits of the Chaplains of the English Church. But early in June fresh symptoms set in, and he became a good deal worse. His sister sat with him in silence, anxious to minister to him. He remained in bed, his nights were more restless, and Dr. Davison had to sleep near him in the Hotel du Rhin.

Lady Victoria, whose truthful mind could not fall in with the usual medical plan of keeping from the invalid his real state, considered it her duty to inform her brother of his very precarious condition. Lord Mornington received the communication with much calmness. His state of health fluctuated a good deal; sometimes he was able even to sit up, but it was apparent that he was altering very much, getting very thin and gradually wasting away. On his sister's next visit Lord Mornington was anxious to know more of the actual truth, and whether his disease was incurable. Lady Victoria had the extremely painful task of telling him the real state of the case, which she did with much distress to her own feelings, but with that faithfulness which always marked her dealings with others. It was evident to Lord Mornington himself that his strength was

failing. He suffered more at night, and at times
fell into a kind of delirium, which was followed by
heavy sleep, from which he woke up excessively
weak. Lady Victoria informed him he had been for
some time prayed for at the English Church. He
still found great solace in his sister's visits, and
confided fully in her. The doctor's opinion was
that Lord Mornington's illness would be a very long
and lingering one, and as just then the weather had
become almost unbearably hot, Lady Victoria
decided on moving to St. Germain, where she
would be more likely to keep in good health by
having the benefit of country air, and be near enough
to her brother to go into Paris to see him when
requisite. So she moved to Villa St. Germain, in
the Rue du Château Neuf, on the 30th of June.
From thence she wrote this letter :—

" Dearest Aunts,—Here I am, very comfortably
established in my little suite of Bijoux holes. My
little drawing-room and two little anterooms not
much larger, but really very comfortably furnished.
No carpets. All the better this hot weather. The
Paris Hotels are all very thickly carpeted now. I
feel so happy to have got out of the noise and heat
of Paris. The Hotel Mirabeau itself is charmingly
quiet, and the apartments I occupied the last three
or four days very cool, but oh ! the streets ! quite
as crowded as London, and the sun about three

times as powerful. I got here about five yesterday, in three-quarters of an hour from Paris. The air so like Malvern, most charming. The dear old Château almost touching the house. I like to suppose this garden must have been part of the Château garden. How I longed for you to be with me yesterday evening. There was such an interesting effect of light through the half-broken, half-ruinous windows of the fine old red-brick building, of course browned by age, and it was so silent and gave me so much to think of. How little can one tell where circumstances will take one to."

In a later letter, from the same address, Lady Victoria wrote to her aunts: "I went on my melancholy pilgrimage yesterday. Our poor, dear invalid always makes the best of himself. Lord Dangan [1] was with him. It is marvellous the successful efforts he makes to appear well before company, but to me the almost instantaneous change of expression and countenance the moment the door closes is sad to see, though I am always rejoiced he is really himself with me. Poor dear fellow, the disease extends fearfully, and he complains of want of appetite and great weakness."

During Lady Victoria's sojourn in and near Paris she saw a good deal of her august relatives, Lord Cowley and his family. Of him, in another letter

[1] Lord Cowley's eldest son.

to her aunts, she said : " I am so glad you are going to, or have written to Lord Cowley. I do not know what I should have done without him and his kind judicious advice. I am very comfortably settled here, in a humble way, and enjoy the charming, bracing, pure air and beautiful views to my heart's content." Cheerfully, however, as Lady Victoria wrote, she felt much the solitude and anxiety of that anxious time. In one of her letters she said : " How gladly would I turn my back on ' La Belle France,' notwithstanding its fine dry climate and some few advantages, to be again in dear, good, honest England, but I believe it will ever be a comfort to me to think I was here when I was." Lady Victoria's faculty for thankfulness is much shown in her letters from St. Germain. She dwelt much on feeling so well and on being so wonderfully supported. Not liking the French *cuisine*, she was quite grateful to find that, at Villa St. Germain, she could be supplied with such an English dish as plain roast chicken. She derived much amusement from her courier with his funny speeches in broken English. When various dishes had been offered to her and rejected, he would say, " Never mind, miladi ! There is a nice little beast coming up presently you will be able to eat." The little beast meaning roast chicken.

Lord Mornington's painful illness continued, and the hour at a time, twice a week, spent by his sister by his dying bed, became more and more precious to her. With the tender love she had ever felt for him, she watched, with acute pain, every change which marked the approach of their separation. She prayed beside him, and did all she could to comfort his declining hours. He was, of course, the one engrossing subject of her thoughts, the object of her affectionate care and solicitude. St. Germain is only three-quarters of an hour's journey by rail from Paris, so Lady Victoria could readily reach the Hotel du Rhin whenever her presence was required. For three weeks she remained there, paying her visit to her brother regularly twice a week. As it often happens in illness, the end came sooner than was expected. On July 24th Lord Mornington became alarmingly worse. When his sister came she found him dozing, but when he opened his eyes, and saw her standing by his bed, he threw his arms round her and drew her down on his shoulder. For some minutes he held her fast, stroking her with his other hand, and calling her "his dear little sister." Then he took fast hold of her hand, pressing it with his poor burning one, and so kept her close to him for nearly an hour. In writing afterwards to her aunts, Lady Victoria said : "To my dying hour, his joyous, warm affectionate greeting of me will be an inexpressible comfort to me." For two days he had recognized no one but his sister and his constant

attendant, Pallaster. The following day, the 25th,
Lady Victoria found him quite unconscious. He
scarcely opened his eyes when she went to him. It
was evident that the end was near, for the sad and
terrible change of colour which precedes death had
passed over his face. When this last sad visit was
over, Lord Cowley, who was there, sent Lady
Victoria to the Embassy in his brougham. Her
maid went to St. Germain to pack up her things
and remove them there. Lady Victoria was told by
Pallaster, the last thing, that Lord Mornington was
thoroughly conscious, and heard him repeat the
Lord's Prayer and another prayer. Before the night
of July 25th had passed, Lord Mornington died.
Thus passed away, in his forty-ninth year, William
Richard Arthur, the fifth Earl of Mornington, the
last who bore that title, and the last male heir of the
House of Tylney Long. The title of Earl of Mornington and the Viscountcy of Wellesley passed to
his cousin, the Duke of Wellington. The Barony
of Maryborough became extinct. Lord Mornington's
only sister, Lady Victoria Long Wellesley, then
became (with the exception of her aunts) the sole
representative of four remarkable families; on her
father's side, the Pole Wellesleys of Ballybin, from
whom she took her title, and on her mother's side, the
Longs of Draycot Cerne, Wilts, the Childs of Wanstead, Essex, and the Tylneys of Tylney Hall, Hants.

Full of sorrow at the loss of her only brother and nearest relative, Lady Victoria nerved herself to the last sad duties before her. In the bright summer weather, and in the lovely "City of Paris," the bereaved lady prepared, with a sad heart, to be escorted by Lord Cowley and the other mourners across the Channel and from London to Draycot Cerne, where the late Earl was to be buried. Before leaving Paris it was found that in his last days Lord Mornington had executed another and a third will. It was necessary to open it before proceeding on the journey. To the astonishment of Lady Victoria and all her friends, her brother, in this last will, left all the estates which had belonged to his mother to his father's first cousin, Lord Cowley. To his steward, Captain Pallaster, he left £500 a year. To his only sister, Lady Victoria, he bequeathed an annuity of £1,000 per annum. The Tylney Long estates, and specially Draycot, (which had belonged to her mother's family for four hundred years), were especially dear to Lady Victoria. It was no wonder, therefore, that she greatly felt this additional trial and disappointment. It was at this juncture that the true Christianity with which her life was imbued, was shown to its highest advantage. With a brave spirit and a resigned will she went through that journey to England, now rendered so doubly sad. For the last time she entered the home of her ancestors. The rain was falling fast, as for the last time she knelt in worship in Draycot Church as her only brother's remains were borne into the family vault. When the painful ceremony was over she left Draycot, never again to return to it until the day when she, as the last of her race, was also borne into her tomb in that ancient Church, to rest in peace in the only niche of ground that remained to her of her mother's vast and princely estates.

When Lady Victoria's first grief at her brother's death was somewhat abated, the loss of Draycot was felt by her more keenly. But the gentleness of her disposition was such, her religious feeling so strong, and her faith in an over-ruling Providence so great, that, in spite of the keenness of her grief, she met the trial with a calmness which was astonishing in one who possessed such very deep feelings. Beautiful indeed was the soul within, that was to be still further purified by such severe trials. Those who saw her in her most unguarded moments, heard no word from her lips which the most censorious could have taken exception to. Her blue eyes would indeed be suffused with tears, but her tongue would utter words of trust, of faith, and of deepest resignation to the will of God. It seemed, at times, as if her spirit were even then half in heaven.

"Lady Victoria has behaved like an angel," exclaimed a young clergyman then officiating in Wilt-

shire. In her there was no morbid looking back to
the past splendours of her family, no repining at the
position she had lost, but rather a cheerful acceptance of whatever of worldly good was left to her.
"I am quite sure," she said, upon one occasion,
"that if 'such and such things' were good for me
God would send them to me." So she passed
through the dark clouds of sorrow and disappointment with a cheerful spirit, which never failed her,
and came forth from them better, purer, and more
angelic than ever. She did not forsake those who
lived on the estate which had passed away from her.
She sent loving messages to such of the people who
could remember her family. Hearing that one
favourite old man, a carpenter named Bevington,
had very little to support him in his declining years,
she sent sums of money to be given to him in weekly
payments, and did so as long as he lived. It seemed
as if, in unselfish care for others, she found, (next to
her trust in God), her best consolation.

Upon receiving a letter describing the affection
expressed for her by the Draycot people, she wrote
in reply :—

"It is very gratifying to know that one is really
cared for by those whose welfare it would have been
one's highest ambition, as well as one's greatest
pleasure, to have promoted. The deprivation of
Draycot is my appointed cross, the burden of which

I can never cease to feel. At the same time I constantly pray to be enabled to bear it with cheerful resignation."

Upon being asked to send her autograph to a lady in the Draycot neighbourhood, Lady Victoria sent it by return of post, with this text written underneath: " Father, Thy will, not mine, be done."

Soon afterwards Lady Victoria entered into some correspondence about placing a window to her brother's memory in Draycot Church. This intention was, however, not carried out. The window in question was eventually placed in South Wraxall Church.

The Misses Long had some new altar rails erected in Draycot Church to the memory of their nephew, with the following inscription and pathetically expressive text :—

IN MEMORY OF

W. R. A. POLE TYLNEY LONG WELLESLEY,

Fifth Earl of Mornington, who died 25th July, 1863,
These Rails are erected by his Maternal Aunts,
Dorothy and Emma Tylney Long.

" I became dumb and opened not my mouth, for it was Thy
doing."

CHAPTER XI.

Severed Ties and New Links.

IN the same year that Lord Mornington died, the Misses Tylney Long, after a residence of about two years at Bolney, determined on again moving. They went to Madehurst Lodge, near Arundel. Lady Victoria had given up her residence at Eastbourne, desiring to settle in a larger house. As she had taken a great fancy to Bolney Lodge, she, with some assistance from her aunts, bought the place.

Bolney,[1] near Cuckfield, is situated in the very centre of Sussex. It is a very pretty place, with nice gardens and shrubberies and a field to its left, which forms a kind of miniature park. Lady Victoria tried to think that it looked a little like Draycot. The place was large enough to enable her to keep an establishment befitting her rank, and yet

[1] George the Fourth, when Prince Regent, used, on his way from London to Brighton, to stay at Bolney Lodge, in order to enjoy the strawberries.

not too large for convenience and comfort. Here
she lived for several years, entertaining her friends
in succession, dispensing hospitality, visiting the
poor, and occupying herself in good works.

At this time Lady Victoria had an income of
£1,900 a year, but she had to visit with county
people possessing from £25,000 to £36,000 a year.
However, she was such an excellent manager that
she could do this with ease and comfort. She was
very fond of furnishing, and every room in her house
was not only in good taste and extremely pretty, but
always had an air of comfort and repose. For all
arrangements were carried out under her own eye.
Never had servants so kind and indulgent a mistress.
For although she was extremely particular, she ruled
her household with the law of love. When she
wished anything done, she spoke deferentially as if
making a request, rather than giving a command.
She earned her reward in that love and devotion
given to her which no payment of service can secure.
From the first days when she started a house of her
own, to the last hours of her life, she was served not
only faithfully, but devotedly and affectionately.
Nothing gave her so much pain as any want of confidence shown in her. If it happened, here and
there, that a servant came who neglected duty or
took any undue advantage, so unusual a circumstance would rather cause her distress than arouse

direct displeasure. At Bolney the faithful Bicknell and his wife were, of course, at the head of her establishment. Her maid, Mary Horne, who had been with her almost from her girlhood, remained, as her faithful and devoted attendant, until the time of her death.

Shortly after the passing away of Draycot, and during her residence at Bolney, Lady Victoria paid several visits to Mr. Walter Long and his second wife, Lady Bishop. Mr. Walter Long's place, Rood Ashton, Wilts, is situated near the old family mansion of South Wraxall. Lady Victoria felt great interest in visiting the old scenes, which had so much to do with the ancient history of her family. The kindness and sympathy with which she was treated at Rood Ashton, greatly supported and consoled her. She formed a friendship with Lady Bishop which lasted until that lady died. At South Wraxall Church, about this time, Lady Victoria put up the window to her brother, Lord Mornington's memory, which helps still further to beautify that old and interesting Church.

Bolney Lodge was well suited for Lady Victoria's requirements. There was a good deal of pleasant society in the neighbourhood. Her nearest neighbours were the Sergessons, of Cuckfield Park, with whom she had much pleasant intercourse. Croquet was then in vogue, and many pleasant parties were given, within twenty miles round, which Lady Victoria often graced with her presence. Her own parties were very pleasant and popular. Her ease and grace as a hostess, spread a charm on all around, infusing an air of geniality and enjoyment into her guests.

Lady Victoria's life at Bolney was very peaceful and pleasant, until one autumn a very sad and surprising circumstance occurred. Her head gardener, who had lived in her aunts' service, and whom she had every reason to trust, was found to have taken advantage of her. Upon further investigation, it was discovered that he had deceived and cheated her in many respects. Lady Victoria summoned him to her presence, and with feelings of great distress at his conduct, pointed out to him his faults and their consequences, if he continued to pursue such courses. She then felt obliged to dismiss him from her service.

Overcome at being found out, at the displeasure of so "kind a mistress," and in despair at losing his situation, he left her presence and took the desperate step of committing suicide. In the morning the unhappy man was found hanging in one of the arbours, quite dead. This painful circumstance had a great effect on Lady Victoria's delicate nerves. For weeks she could not sleep. At last, thinking that Bolney did not agree with her, she, when Christmas drew near, formed the resolution of giving up the place, and seeking in other air to recover her health. She left Bolney somewhat suddenly. She tried Worthing and other places for her health, as for some time she was very unwell. Later on she bought Brunswick House, at her favourite Eastbourne, removed her family pictures and furniture there, and let Bolney on a long lease. One of the special works she took up about that time was the " United Kingdom Beneficent Society," for granting pensions to ladies in reduced circumstances. She acted as local secretary for this Society, and took great interest in collecting money for it. She entered into a good deal of correspondence about it with the late Mrs. Leicester, of Onega Lodge, Bath.

In the December of 1872 Lady Victoria lost her eldest aunt, Miss Tylney Long. She was staying at Madehurst when the sad event occurred, which took away one who had been as a mother to her. Miss Long had risen as usual, and was in the course of dressing when she sat down and almost immediately expired. This was Lady Victoria's own account :—

" My dearest Aunt Dora entered her blissful rest last Friday morning about eight o'clock, with very little previous warning, and so painlessly and without one struggle her dear affectionate heart ceased to beat, and in an instant the released and bright spirit was in its eternal and glorious home. We

I

cannot wish her back again in this world of sin and
sorrow, but it is terrible to be here without her
affectionate, loving presence. The sad ceremony
takes place Friday, I believe, at Draycot, and I am
thankful dearest Aunt Emma does not attempt the
sad journey. Of course I remain with her."

The sisters had been so inseparable all their lives,
that it was almost supposed that the one could not
exist without the other. But where real affection
exists there is no bitterness in grief, and Miss Emma
Long, with her real Christianity, resigned herself to
the parting with her beloved sister in the " sure and
certain hope " of meeting her again in a happier
world.

Miss Emma survived her sister for some years.
In 1877, or about that time, her health became so
weak and enfeebled that Lady Victoria felt it
necessary to be almost entirely with her at Madehurst Lodge. She therefore went there, with a few
of her servants, and devoted herself to ministering
to the comfort of her last remaining near relative.
For some years Miss Long remained in a weak and
uncertain state of health. Very different to her
sainted sister's rapid removal was the sad and
lingering illness she had to undergo. Lady Victoria
was wonderfully supported through these years of
watching and anxiety. It was during her residence
at Madehurst that she contracted a very strong

friendship with Mr. John Long and his family, of
the Firs, Arundel. They were descended from the
Prushaw Longs, who came from the same stock as
the ancient Longs of Wraxall and Draycot. Being
so peculiarly without near relatives, and with the
approaching loss of her only remaining aunt before
her, it was but natural that Lady Victoria should
turn to those who bore her mother's name, with all
the affection of her loving nature. It was also a
great comfort to her through the long seclusion,
consequent upon Miss Emma Long's illness, to have
those at hand who could sympathize with her
anxiety, and with whom she could exchange frequent
and friendly meetings. It so happened while Lady
Victoria was staying at Madehurst that West Stoke,
a very pretty and desirable place on the Goodwood
estate, became vacant. Lady Victoria was advised
to take the opportunity of securing this place for her
own residence. She looked upon this, as she did
on all the events of life, as a special Providence
directing her steps for the future.

After visiting West Stoke and feeling very much
pleased with it, she decided on taking it on a long
lease from the Duke of Richmond. As Miss Emma
Long had now become a confirmed invalid, for the
most of her time scarcely conscious, and as it was
considered injurious for Lady Victoria's always
delicate health to continue her attendance upon the

invalid, she determined on removing to her new residence as soon as it was ready for her habitation. West Stoke is a small village, prettily situated on the Chichester road. Near it is Kingly Bottom, with its immense and ancient yew trees. There is a tradition that fairies have haunted this spot. At all events, it has a strange and weird appearance, especially by moonlight.

Beyond Kingly Bottom, rises Bow Hill on the Sussex Downs, from whence very pure air can be obtained. This hill was a favourite walk of the late Bishop of Chichester. West Stoke House is a very old building. The interior is built in the form of a cross. There are several staircases. One staircase leads to a separate set of rooms. These were Lady Victoria's private apartments. There is one enormous state-bedroom, such as is often seen in old houses, and many others of different sizes. The drawing-room was a charming room, leading out into a conservatory beyond. The dining-room is a handsome size, and the portraits of Lady Victoria's ancestors, hung on the walls, gave it an imposing appearance. There was a library, which contained many of the Draycot books. There were also other smaller rooms on the ground floor. It was altogether a larger and handsomer house than Lady Victoria had ever had before. Her exquisite taste in furnishing made all the rooms look extremely

WEST STOKE HOUSE,

ON THE GOODWOOD ESTATE.

pretty and tempting.   Blue was her favourite colour.
The drawing-room carpet was blue, and the curtain
of blue silk.   The couches and chairs were uphol-
stered with amber.   There is a glass door leading
from the hall into the flower garden and lawn
beyond.   There were many choice shrubs on the
lawn.   In one corner stood a most beautiful cork
tree, high as an ordinary elm.   It was propped up
for very age.   Passing from the lawn to the left you
came upon a tempting walk, which was so sunny
and warm, even in winter, that once a butterfly was
found there on Christmas Day.   From this walk, on
a clear day, you could see the Isle of Wight.   A
little way on was a good sized kitchen garden, and
close to it the little farm.   Part of the grounds
belonging to the house were laid out in shrubberies,
which were very delightful, with their grassy walks
overhung with nut bushes.   The neighbourhood is
quiet and secluded.   At night owls might be heard
screeching, and seen flying freely about.   Round the
front of the house was a beautiful magnolia, whose
blossoms seemed as if they kissed the windows.   One
beautiful solitary blossom might sometimes be seen
upon it at Christmas time.

The Church is close to the house.   At that time
it had the old-fashioned high-backed pews with doors.
It was restored with open pews under the present
incumbent, the Rev. William F. Shaw. Lady Victoria

undertook the expenses of these improvements.

The village consists of only about one hundred inhabitants. Of these a good many were Lady Victoria's outdoor servants, who occupied several of the cottages. The farm, belonging to the estate, was a great interest to Lady Victoria. In the business connected with this larger place, she felt much indebted to Mr. Long of the Firs, who came over to West Stoke, from time to time, to confer with and advise her. Mrs. Long also frequently visited her at West Stoke. This place was within a drive of her aunt's residence, so that Lady Victoria was able frequently to go over to see her last near relative, whose sad and lingering illness continued for about a year after Lady Victoria settled at West Stoke. For in the July of the following summer Miss Long became materially worse, and on the 16th of that month the end came, about which Lady Victoria wrote from Madehurst : " The sad event, shall I call it, has taken place which we have so long expected, and my dearest aunt is taken to her blessed rest. She has had two or three bad attacks of difficulty of breathing since this day week, and I remained here till yesterday afternoon. From the report I had from her nurse late yesterday afternoon, I should have come here to-day, at all events. About half past eight this morning, my maid came in with the sad intelligence that a messenger had come over from Madehurst. My dear aunt passed off in her sleep, with scarcely a sigh and not a struggle. A blessed end to a most holy life."

The funeral of this, the last remaining daughter of Sir James and Lady Catherine Long, took place also at Draycot Cerne.

CHAPTER XII.

A Great Work.

UPON the death of Miss Emma Long, Lady Victoria, as their only near relative, came into the fortunes of both her aunts. For by Miss Long's will her fortune had been left to her sister for her life, to pass, after her death, to her niece. Miss Emma Long left her's absolutely to Lady Victoria, with the exception, of course, of certain legacies. So she became, at last, very wealthy. Into no better or wiser hands could this accumulated money have come.

For Lady Victoria, who had learnt so early the sweet lessons of adversity, made it her primary aim to do good. The first fruits of her fortune were to be set apart for the noble work of building a Church, dedicated to the glory of God and the memory of her beloved aunts. She set to work most zealously, with all the care and thought which was needed for so great an undertaking. She also multiplied her subscriptions to many benevolent objects. She never turned away from any claim upon her purse, great or small. Wherever money was needed, money was cheerfully and readily given.

For many years she had been silently and steadily engaged in good works. She had never been "weary of well doing." One who had so dedicated her life to God, who had yielded to His service the first fruits of her youth, was surely well fitted for the holy work on which her heart was set. She felt like David, "The house that is to be builded for the Lord my God must be exceeding magnifical,"[1] and she laid her plans accordingly. The site for the Church she intended to build, was given by the Duke of Devonshire. It was in the Susan's Road, in the midst of the new streets and squares which had recently been built in that and the Tideswell Road, where the population consists, for the most part, of working classes. The situation is at once central and commanding, and is some little distance from the sea. The site was formerly a cricket field, lying below the level of the town drainage. To get over this difficulty a good deal of expense had to be incurred. Messrs. Parr and Strong, the architects, caused foundations more than twenty feet in depth to be put in down to the solid rock, and had a floor or platform constructed above the level of the road-way, upon which the new Church was to be erected.

[1] 1 Chron. xxii. 5.

It had been a matter of great consideration to
Lady Victoria's conscientious mind as to whom she
should appoint as vicar to the new parish.   Through
her young relative, the Rev. Alfred Long, younger
son of Mr. John Long, of the Firs, she heard a good
deal of the Rev. John Brunsdon Fletcher, of St.
Paul's, Edinburgh, to whom Mr. Long was curate.
After a good deal of that prayerful consideration,
without which no undertaking of Lady Victoria's
was ever carried out, she decided on offering the
Church to Mr. Fletcher.   It was accepted.   The
deep interest which he and Mrs. Fletcher felt in this
Church was shown by their taking a house in a
situation which enabled them to watch the building
of the sacred edifice, from the first stone to the last.
The style fixed upon was the " Lombard Byzantine."
There is at present only one other Church in the
kingdom built in the purity of that style, and that is
the Parish Church at Wilton, near Salisbury.

The corner stone was laid by Bishop Durnford, on
the 14th of June, 1881.   The walls were then about
ten feet high, so that a foundation stone, in the
strict sense of the word, was not possible.   There
was a very large assembly of the local clergy and
friends at the ceremony.

After the customary office had been said, the re-
sponses were sung by the choir of St. Saviour's.
Various coins of the realm, and a parchment setting

forth the date of the ceremonial, etc., having been deposited beneath the stone, it was lowered into its proper position, and his Lordship having set it with a silver trowel, declared it to be properly laid. In the course of an address to the assembled crowd, the Bishop said : " I wish you all to understand that I appear here to-day as the deputed representative of a noble lady, to whom this place and neighbourhood are so largely indebted. We have good reason to thank Almighty God for having put it into the heart of. Lady Victoria Long Wellesley to raise, at such vast expense, this Church, which is designed for the benefit of the Christian population which surrounds it. We all feel, we all desire to express, the sense we entertain of this disinterested resolution on her part. She builds a noble temple to the Almighty God, and, as we trust, to the honour of His holy name and the enlargement of His kingdom. She builds it in a place with which she has no material connection, being moved only by the necessities of the people, being only desirous of doing all the good she can with large means. It is that which has interested her to provide further that this noble Church, when it pleases God,—as I trust it soon will do—that it shall stand in its place, shall be opened to all the inhabitants of this district, without distinction and without reservation, and the minister of Christ—for whom she has also made provision—will invite all to come in, and will preach to them the words of salvation from the gospel of the Lord. This Church has not been built on this floor without many difficulties. You know the soil on which it stands is a most treacherous one, and, at a great cost, the architect has been obliged to go down to the solid rock in order to obtain a secure foundation. That foundation, he assures me, has been obtained, and this Church, as far as he can see, may stand for ages a monument of the liberality of its founder, and a blessing to the people. In this matter it is but a pattern and figure of the Church spiritual of Christ, which also is built on no sandy or insecure foundation, but erected never to fall, and the gates of hell shall never prevail against it."

His Lordship concluded by hoping that, as the intentions of the founder were that the Church would be a blessing to the neighbours and to the inhabitants, so the latter would, by their piety and improvement in all holiness and good living, evince their sense of gratitude to Almighty God, and also, through Him, to her whose munificence they that day celebrated. He ventured to say that in her absence which he would not say in her presence—and he believed there was not a single person in the assembly present who would not respond to her wishes—that she might see that Church raised to be a blessing to the neighbourhood and to the people. The ceremony concluded by the singing of a hymn and the Benediction pronounced by the Bishop.

The incumbent designate of All Souls' was the Rev. J. P. Fletcher, M.A., late incumbent of St. Paul's, Edinburgh, and then (1882) residing at Edinburgh House, Blackwater Road, Eastbourne. The architects were Messrs. Parr and Strong, Finsbury Square, London, and Mr. J. Peerless, of Eastbourne, was the builder. The external dimensions are one hundred and twenty-seven feet from east to west and sixty-eight feet from north to south, and fifty-one feet in height to the ridge of the nave. The internal dimensions of the nave are eighty-six feet six inches from east to west, and the height thirty-three feet, and thirty-nine feet to the plate, or forty-nine feet to the top of the open timber roof. The north and south aisles each eighty-six feet six inches by thirteen feet, and eighteen feet to the plate, or twenty-six feet to top of lean-to roof. The chancel is separated from the nave by an " Arcus Triumphalis," twenty-four feet in width by thirty-seven feet in height, the heights being nineteen feet, thirty-three feet, and thirty-eight feet to the wooden ceiling. The apse is of twelve feet radius, and is lighted by seven windows. There is a lofty stone semi-dome and reredos in Caen stone. The north chancel aisle, enclosed, forms an admirable vestry. The south chancel aisle, nineteen feet by thirteen feet, forms a grand position for the magnificent organ [by Bishop and Son, London]. The Church is calculated to seat eight hundred persons. The nave arcades consist of seven arches on each side, with clerestory windows over. At the west of the Church there is a wheel window, nine feet in diameter. The principal materials used for the outside are red bricks from Keymer and buff from Tamworth, with red and buff dressings of terracotta, by Gibbs and Canning, of Tamworth. The inside facings are Burnham bricks with stone dressings—white and blue Horsham—prepared by Messrs. Farmer and Brindley, of London. The campanile at the south-west corner, which is connected with the Church by a short arcade, is sixteen feet square and eighty-three feet in height. It contains a clock with four faces, and a peal of bells above. The style of the building is Lombard Byzantine, of the end of the sixth century, as seen at Crema, Verona, Ravenna, etc. It may be stated that the lady donor was an occasional resident at Brunswick House, Eastbourne, in which town she has always shown much interest. The structure was commenced in 1879, and its foundations alone cost about four thousand pounds. It is erected in memory of the lady relatives of the giver, namely, her aunts, Dorothy and Emma Tylney Long.

Of all the subjects that engrossed Lady Victoria's active mind, the building of her beautiful Church was, naturally, of the deepest interest to her. But while it was in progress, she fulfilled all other duties faithfully and wisely. At West Stoke, as at Bolney, she showed great hospitality both in receiving visitors to stay with her, and in giving entertainments to the neighbourhood, in which she made many pleasant friends. Her relations with the Palace and the Cathedral clergy of Chichester were of a very pleasant kind. That most interesting man, Dean Burgon, was a great friend of hers. She took real interest in the villagers at West Stoke, visiting them personally whenever she could. The tiny Village School was a great interest to her. When she first resided at West Stoke, she would go to it every week to give a Bible lesson to the children. Every year she gave the girls new red cloaks, and black hats trimmed with red. She retained a love for old customs ; so the boys were dressed in the old-fashioned smock frocks, and very nice and clean they looked. It was a pretty sight to see the children trooping to Church, especially on a cold Christmas day, the red cloaks of the girls making a line of bright colour over the snow. And it was a very hearty service which was held, on Christmas Day, in the little Church at West Stoke. It was Lady Victoria's delight to receive the school children at her house on the afternoon of Christmas Day. She would come into the hall, (warm with its cheerful wood fire), to welcome them, with her face beaming with smiles. The children would then stand round her and sing their Christmas carols. Then, with her own hands, she would give each child a bun and a penny. One of the smallest of the boys once burst into tears, because he had received twopence by mistake, and had to resign one of the pennies. He was taken into the kitchen, where a large slice of plum pudding soon consoled him.

On one occasion the children were about to have an extra treat. They were invited to a Christmas tree, which was to be loaded with presents. In the meantime, however, one of the carters in Lady Victoria's employ was taken suddenly ill and died. Out of respect to this poor man's memory, Lady Victoria thought proper to put aside the entertainment. So the presents were indeed given, though there was no Christmas tree to put them on. Each Christmas Eve the mummers would come, according to old custom, and serenade the Lady of West Stoke. On New Year's Day they were admitted into the hall to sing to her.

She greatly loved entertaining the little cripples from "The Cripples' Home" at Bognor. Twice a year, in summer on her lawn, and in winter in her hall, they were received by her to have some hours of their poor little helpless lives brightened by her kindness. Her benevolence and her genuineness and sincerity of character were apparent in all her dealings, while her bright and cheerful temperament and her charming manners delighted all who came near her. When she entered the room it seemed like the coming in of a sunbeam. When any mention of Draycot came up, her face would wear an expression of sadness, but a second or so afterwards she would make some cheerful observation which showed her trust in Providence and her belief that "all was for the best." Her Church views were always pure and orthodox, and she would exhort those she loved to cling to the pure teaching of our Church. The most advanced in holiness are ever the lowliest in spirit. Lady Victoria Wellesley was a striking example of true Christian humility. It was so natural to her to be kind that she thought but little of what she did for others. It was so much the habit of her mind to be devout and religious, that to her in the best sense of the phrase "habit was second nature." She once wrote: "We can do nothing without the daily, or rather the hourly, prayer for the Holy Spirit." It may be said of her that her life was a prayer, for she did nothing, she gave no advice without first asking for Divine guidance. One instance of her humility may be

K

given. One of her god-daughters illuminated a Christmas card for her with this text: " Her price is far above rubies." Lady Victoria wrote back: "I cannot accept your card. It is too high praise for *me*. So I have put it amongst the cards sent to my aunt."

While Lady Victoria passed her time quietly and peacefully at West Stoke, the Church at Eastbourne was making rapid progress. While it was in course of building, Sunday services were held by the vicar-designate in the Holy Trinity school-room, kindly lent by the vicar of Holy Trinity and licensed by the Bishop. In this way the beginning of a congregation was formed and a choir trained, ready for the Consecration Day.

On the 6th of July, 1882, a little more than a year from the laying of the corner stone, the Church was consecrated by Bishop Durnford.

Lady Victoria was, of course, present herself on the day of the Consecration, and felt a profound and sacred satisfaction and pleasure at the completion of her beautiful and holy work, the fulfilment of her heart's desire.

It was truly a fitting memorial, from a living saint, to the saintly relatives who had preceded her to their eternal Home.

At the west end of the Church Lady Victoria placed a brass plate with this inscription :—

ALL SOULS' CHURCH, EASTBOURNE.

To the Glory of God,
For the good of All Souls,
And in loving and most grateful memory of
The excellent ladies,
DOROTHY AND EMMA TYLNEY LONG,
This Church is erected.
Consecrated by
Richard Durnford, D.D., Lord Bishop of Chichester,
The 6th day of July, 1882.

Round this tablet, in letters so placed that they could scarcely be distinguished, the donor of the Church allowed her one name "Victoria" to be inserted. She had a window put up to the memory of Miss Emma Long as the centre light of the apse. The subject is "The Good Shepherd." In the panels of the apse the verses are enshrined in mosaics of the twenty-third Psalm, which afforded Miss Emma Long so much comfort in her last illness and which she was never tired of repeating.

The Church has the appropriate name of "All Souls," as a Church for everyone. The interior of the edifice is most beautiful in all its details.

The dome is constructed of the finest Bath stone, and into the centre the figure of the Holy Dove with rays is inserted in mosaics. At the time of the final decoration of the sanctuary, the vault of the dome was coloured a soft blue, through which the joints of the stonework are perceptible ; the principle of the ornamentation being, not to *conceal* the structural work, but to beautify it ; and elsewhere in the decorations the texture of the underlying material, whether brick or stone, is clearly shown.

The original sum set apart by Lady Victoria Wellesley amounted to about £22,500. But as the Church grew under the hands of the architect more and more costly, Lady Victoria added at one time £7,000, and from time to time such other sums as were needed.

The arrangements for building the permanent Vicarage House beside the Church were a little complicated, but *virtually* she *did* build it ; and she gave £1,200 towards the building of the Schools. Schools were not contemplated at first, but the conviction grew upon her that the parochial machinery was not complete without Schools ; hence her generous gift.

All Souls' Church, built and endowed as a special memorial to her beloved aunts, will be to future generations a very beautiful memento of Lady Victoria Long Wellesley herself. Amongst the choice and lovely things in that Church there is one which carries with it a most touching remembrance. It is the kneeler for communicants at the altar step, with vine leaves on a crimson ground, most beautifully worked by Lady Victoria herself. Carefully preserved and reverently handled, it will long remain as the handiwork of the industrious fingers of the noble founder of the Parish and Church of All Souls.

This lovely Church, on which so much care was bestowed, reminds one of the Church of Broue in France, also built by a lady, about which Matthew Arnold wrote such a beautiful poem. I quote the words concerning this Church from a lecture given at Bath, in which it was so described : " And a beautiful structure indeed came from the brains of the builder and the heart of the lady."

CHAPTER XIII.

Light at Eventide.

WEST STOKE became to Lady Victoria, in a smaller way, what Draycot might have been. She found in the little village many interests and much scope for usefulness. The increase of wealth gave her increased opportunities of benevolence, and many and various were the charities she aided. " Money makes money," she once observed, and with her money increased rather than diminished. " The liberal soul shall be made fat," and, while her purse was always open for the wants of others, she was surrounded, in her quiet home, with comfort and luxury. But no earthly possession could ever have made her otherwise than unselfish. About three years after she had settled at West Stoke an outbreak of diphtheria occurred, which took away several young lives and caused her much distress. She very much appreciated the devotion to the sick in his parish shown by the rector. Fearless for his own safety, and thinking only of the

sufferers, the Rev. W. F. Shaw went amongst them
with untiring zeal. Most fortunately the infectious
disease did no harm to him or his. The occasion
was marked by a testimonial, in the shape of a
handsome Bible, accompanied with an address,
which was presented to Mr. Shaw by his parishioners.
The presentation took place in Lady Victoria's own
hall on New Year's Day, where her guests and some
of the leading parishioners assembled to do honour
to the event. It was a question which looked the
most pleased on that occasion, Mr. Shaw or Lady
Victoria herself! Shortly after she settled at West
Stoke her cousin, Mr. John Long, the eldest son of
Mr. Long, of the Firs, married another cousin, Miss
Blanche Penruddocke, from Wilts. Lady Victoria
took a heartfelt interest in this marriage, and lent
them her home for the honeymoon.

During Lady Victoria's residence at West Stoke
she became a Dame of the Primrose League. She
had always been, as her ancestors were before her, a
strict conservative. But she may be said to have
taken a more decided part in politics in later years,
when so many fresh innovations took place. The
idea of the Disestablishment of the Welsh Church
was, of course, specially distasteful to her, and she
worked hard in distributing leaflets against it.

Owing to her delicacy of health Lady Victoria
never travelled much. Her only visits to the Con-

tinent were confined to when she was abroad in her
childhood, and that one sad visit to Paris to be with
her brother, Lord Mornington, in his last days.
Once she spent a very pleasant time in North Wales,
making Penmaenmawr her headquarters. But lovely
as was the summer weather, she caught cold one
evening driving with her friends, when the mist
arose from the mountains. On another occasion,
being always a bad sleeper, she suffered from the
noise and bustle of the first hotel she stopped at,
and decided on relinquishing her proposed tour.

With a delicate throat, and never having been
very strong, she suffered much from any unwonted
fatigue, and frequently caught colds which laid her
up. It was, therefore, remarkable that she was able
to do so much. She worked hard at her various
charities. She personally supervised nearly everything that was done at West Stoke. She had a vast
number of correspondents and, excepting very occasionally, she wrote all her letters herself. She wrote
a bold and beautiful hand. She would emerge from
her morning's retirement with her hands full of the
letters she had written. She possessed the art of
writing interesting and natural letters. She would
enter fully into any subject that impressed her.
Indeed her pen was never idle. She would fill up
the spaces of her time with very beautiful needle-
work. She took up straw-plaiting, did it to perfec-

THE LADY VICTORIA LONG WELLESLEY.

tion and turned out the most lovely little baskets to be sold at bazaars. She was very fond of reading, and although her eyes were never over strong, she was a thoroughly well-read woman. She kept the poor people's library at West Stoke well supplied with books, and took much interest in selecting them. Lady Victoria was very musical, but her hand was such a small one that it could not grasp an octave. Therefore she did not attain to much execution in playing the piano. But she was especially fond of the harmonium, on which she played with great expression. While at Bolney she had a harmonium, more like a small organ, built on purpose for her. "This instrument," observed a gentleman who was staying in the house, "should be called the Victoria Organ."

Lady Victoria, from her delicate health and from her difficulty in sleeping, was, of necessity, a late riser. There are exceptions to every rule, and late rising does not always mean little work. For she was more awake and did more work in her short day than many people got through in their long ones. With her there was no hurry or distraction, for she always kept the even balance of a well regulated mind.

Lady Victoria's powers of superintending both a small and a large household were remarkable. There are very few people who can do both. With the greatest possible liberality, there was in her household no waste. One thing which she did might serve as an example to people of far less means, and often prevent housekeepers getting into difficulties. When she started her first house at Eastbourne, she made an exact calculation of all probable expenses for each six months. Every item was jotted down, from the bread bill to the cost of her pony carriage, and carefully added up.

At Bolney, and, of course, still more at West Stoke, her expenditure came to a great deal more; but the same rules both of economy and liberality prevailed. At West Stoke her own farm supplied her household, and she used to observe she had everything from it but beef.

After the death of her valued butler, Bicknell, Lady Victoria was some time before she could supply his place. At last, after several changes, she was fortunate enough to secure the services of Alfred Lee. He became quite as attentive and almost as attached to her as her faithful Bicknell, and he remained in her service to the end of her life.

Occupied as Lady Victoria was in important and serious matters, few people were able so thoroughly to unbend as she was. She was very fond of games, and liked to enliven her evenings by playing them with her friends. One great point with her was her readiness to be amused. She so thoroughly entered into any bit of innocent fun.[1] She was specially fond of riddles. She would guess them readily, and often made them herself.

As years advanced, she found the climate of Eastbourne too cold. She then took a great fancy to Bournemouth. She bought a house there on the East Cliff, calling it De Crespigny, after her great aunt, Lady Sarah De Crespigny. The milder air of Bournemouth suited her, and she used to go there, as she formerly did to Eastbourne, in spring and autumn. But, after a time, she grew tired of Bournemouth and sold her house there.

Lady Victoria's London residence for some years was 21, Wimpole Street. At this house she had an unfortunate fall. Her foot slipped, and she fell down a whole flight of stairs. This accident she never entirely got over, and it had the effect of causing her some difficulty in walking. In 1893 she purchased 59, Portland Place. As usual, she took much interest in furnishing this house and making it as pretty as possible. In the last years of Lady

[1] The simple ways of her old governess, Mdlle. de Joux, caused her much good-natured merriment. She once had the beautiful white tail of one of her dead ponies dressed to hang in the hall. When it came back from the furrier's, Mdlle. de Joux regarded it attentively, and then rushed to the stable, thinking it was meant as a false tail for the white pony who drew the small carriage. The dear old lady returned, exclaiming : " Mais il a deja une très bonne queue."

Victoria's life she kept to these two residences in London and West Stoke, going from one to the other, and not attempting the spring and autumn move to the seaside as formerly. For many years she had left off attending the Drawing-rooms and mixing in the parties of the London world. Her visits to town were quiet ones, and she mostly confined herself to the society of a few intimate friends. In fact, so quietly had Lady Victoria lived that in a paper on Wanstead read at the Leyton Literary Club in 1894 the writer of it stated that Mrs. Long Wellesley had only left two children. However modest Lady Victoria might be, she was not inclined to have her existence entirely ignored in the village which adjoined the princely property her mother had owned. So she wrote the following letter to the writer of the paper in question. It was published in one of the Essex newspapers.

"*59, Portland Place, W.,*
"*October 23rd,* 1894.

"Sir,—I have seen in a provincial paper that you have been lecturing recently at the Leyton Literary Club on Wanstead House and Park. Permit me to remark that you made a mistake in saying my beloved mother 'left only two children.' I am her only daughter, and I had two brothers, who both died unmarried some years ago. My own experience is the last chapter of a most unhappy history. My last surviving brother willed me, many years before his death, what remained of my dear mother's property, and this was not inconsiderable, including our dearly-loved ancestral home in Wiltshire ; but within a few days of his decease he completed another will, leaving all to the second Lord Cowley, our father's first cousin. You are also under one or two other incorrect impressions. Thus, my grandfather, Sir James Tylney Long, left one son and three daughters, of whom my dear mother was the eldest. My little uncle, the last baronet, died under age, when my mother became the richest heiress in England, and I was brought up by her two sisters. My dear mother never was Lady Catherine Long. She died the Hon. Mrs. Long Wellesley. Her mother, my grandmother, was Lady Catherine Long, daughter of the Earl of Plymouth. You will see my birth mentioned under the collateral branches of the Duke of Wellington's family, my father and eldest brother having successively succeeded to the Earldom of Mornington.

" For many years my dear brother intended that I should have taken my mother's place as owner of what yet remained of her princely property, my youngest brother having died ; and so it ought to have been. Myself and my two brothers were born at Wanstead House. It is a heartfelt gratification to me to hear that my dear mother is not forgotten. She was indeed worthy of all respect and affection.

"With many thanks,
"Believe me,
"Yours very faithfully,
"V. Long Wellesley."

The last days of a life that had begun under such strange vicissitudes, were calm and happy ones. Lady Victoria had risen above her misfortunes. She had proved that this world's possessions were but little, compared to the glorious inheritance in store for her above. She may be said to have enjoyed life, and to have been full of life to the last, and yet to have always stood in readiness to leave it. Death to her calm and gentle spirit had no terror, and she never minded alluding to her own departure from this world. "I have passed the allotted span," she said, in writing to one of her god-daughters, to acknowledge her congratulations on her birthday. Many of her friends, some older and some younger than herself, passed away from her one by one.

Dean Burgon, whose friendship she had much enjoyed and who had often visited at her house, was called to his rest. Her kind neighbour, Mrs. Durnford, died. She was followed not many years

afterwards by her husband, the reverend and aged
Bishop of Chichester, Dr. Durnford. His grave
was lined with pure white flowers, sent by Lady
Victoria from the West Stoke Conservatories. Mr.
and Mrs. John Long, of the Firs, had passed away.
Lady Victoria felt much sorrow at parting from one
of her oldest friends, who had often been a great
comfort to her, Miss Rich, daughter of Sir George
Rich. Many others whom she had known in youth,
or become attached to in later years, had parted from
her years ago. Lady Victoria accepted with resignation each trial of parting as it came, and diligently
kept on in her own course of benevolence and usefulness with unflagging energy.

The Victoria Home for convalescent women and
girls, which she had built and endowed at Bognor,
was a great source of interest to her. In the July
of 1896 she wrote, " My little Convalescent Home at
Bognor gives me a great deal of correspondence, but
I am thankful to say it is very flourishing, and I have
daily requests for admissions. Many return there
once and even three times, so it shows they are
happy." A few months before, Lady Victoria had
been engaged in having a favourite Book of Devotions
printed, in larger type, for her own use and for presents
to her special friends. In July it was ready, and I
think it may be considered almost her last work. It
is entitled " Private Devotions." The prayers are

well chosen and most appropriate for daily use. In
the August of that year, she was occupied in finding
out and copying any notices she could find of her
family, with a view to some description being placed
under each of the family portraits. It was strange
how her mind went back to the past history of her
family in this, the last year of her earthly existence.
One of her god-daughters having sent her some
notice from a newspaper of the Tylney family, she
wrote back : " The Tylney history was very interesting, but if you have an opportunity I wish you would
inform the writer that the family is not quite extinct,
as the only daughter of the Mrs. Long Wellesley he
mentions is still alive, though an old woman, under
the name of Lady V. Tylney Long Wellesley, her
father having succeeded to the Earldom of Mornington after her mother's death."

Some information about Draycot having been sent
her from the same source, she in reply, spoke of the
loss of Draycot as " the greatest sorrow of her life."
That last autumn Lady Victoria did not feel strong
enough to make the customary visit to London on
business, as she had done in former years. So she
judged it wiser to remain in her comfortable home
at West Stoke. Her health was seen perceptibly to
fail, and for some time she was carried upstairs to
bed every evening. Since her return from London
in July, she had only driven out in her carriage once

or twice. Later on she had attacks of giddiness, and her personal attendants were afraid to leave her alone for long. Some one had to sleep in her room every night. She was carefully and lovingly tended. Her happy spirit of contentment never failed her, and she was always cheerful and pleased with those about her. Notwithstanding so many signs of weakness, no one, not even her medical attendant, thought that the end of her life was so near.

L

CHAPTER XIV.

The Last of Her Race.

IN the March of 1897, Lady Victoria lost another old and valued friend and neighbour, Sir Craven Goring. When on Saturday, the 20th, the Rector of West Stoke called upon her, soon after Sir Craven's funeral, she expressed to him a presentiment she had as to the mode of her own death. This seemed like a foreshadowing of what was to be, for it occurred to her within a week of her last and sudden illness. On the following Friday, the 26th, she came down as usual. She sat down to her morning's occupation of writing. For some years the organist, Miss Nellie Russell, had acted as her secretary. Sometimes Maria Nicholas, who had done everything for her in the parish, addressed her letters for her. The last letter she wrote was to one of her cousins. When Maria asked if she should address that letter for her, Lady Victoria exclaimed, " Oh, no ! I must address it myself, or she will be so alarmed." So her last recorded words were full of her customary care and consideration for others. It may be interesting to mention that one of the last papers to which she affixed her signature, was an admission for a poor man to a Convalescent Home at Seaford. About half an hour before her luncheon she had a visit from her medical attendant, Dr. Buckell, who noticed nothing unusual about her.

Having finished her morning's work, she went into the dining-room and commenced her luncheon, little thinking it was her last meal. Soon afterwards, she requested her butler to fetch her some little thing she had forgotten to bring in with her. He left the room to do so. Before he could return he heard the sound of a fall. He hastened into the room and, to his surprise and distress, he found his beloved mistress on the floor. Assistance was summoned and they raised her up. She just spoke once and then relapsed into semi-unconsciousness. Little thought the household of West Stoke, when they rose that morning, that at three o'clock in the afternoon their gentle lady would be stricken down, never to speak again. But such a sudden summons to one whose life had been " hid with God," seemed more like translation than ordinary death. All that could be done was immediately done. Dr. Buckell and his son were in attendance. The rector, Mr. Shaw came to her at once. He found her conscious, though unable to speak or move. Her legal adviser, Mr. Whitehead, was telegraphed for. He at once telegraphed to town for Sir William Broadbent or Sir Douglas Powell. The former arrived at West Stoke as soon as possible. He gave no hope of her recovery, and considered she might only linger for a few days. On Saturday, Mr. Shaw came and read the twenty-third Psalm by her bedside. She seemed then insensible. So, getting gradually weaker, she lay on in painless unconsciousness. Her bright and loving spirit had nearly reached her Eternal Home, but the body she no longer needed lay still and immoveable. She just recognized the sound of a voice, but that was all.

On Monday, March 29th, (exactly two months before her seventy-ninth birthday), at four o'clock in the morning, she passed peacefully away. She never regained consciousness, and as far as the doctors could judge, she suffered no pain. So, mercifully spared the pain and weariness of a long illness, as quietly as a child in its mother's arms, Lady Victoria's spirit sank into the sleep of death. It was a fitting close to a holy and active life.

No pen can describe the sorrow that was felt at her death. Wherever the name of Lady Victoria Wellesley was known, that name was associated with deeds and words of benevolence and kindness. Wherever that name could do good she had allowed it to be used ; but, of a great part of her charities, she did not "let her left hand know what her right hand did." Far and near the intelligence of her death was received by all her friends with the deepest grief. Rich and poor alike deplored her loss. The villagers of West Stoke missed a warm and sincere friend, her household the kindest of mistresses. They did not dare to tell the poor man, whom Lady Victoria's almost last signature had admitted into the Home, lest the loss of his benefactress should upset him too much.

At Eastbourne, as the knell of All Souls' sounded its repeated notes of sadness, one of the parishioners there exclaimed, " Oh ! can that be for Lady Victoria ? " Yes, it was indeed for her. Never again would those kind lips utter their words of love. Never again would that kind hand unclasp the ready purse, or its warm pressure be felt. Alas ! how little do we know how close we may be to the " never mores " of life.

The funeral of Lady Victoria Wellesley was fixed for the following Friday, April 2nd. It was her express wish to be buried with her near relatives and her ancestors in Draycot Cerne Church. Permission was obtained from the Home Office for the family vault of the Draycot Longs to be opened, to receive this last descendant of their ancient line. So preparations were made for the sad journey.

But first, on the day before, Thursday, April 1st,
a most impressive Memorial Service was held in
West Stoke Church.   The following account of this
Service, together with the pathetic notice of the
lamented lady, appeared in one of the Sussex
papers :—

"WEST STOKE.

"THE LATE LADY VICTORIA LONG WELLESLEY.—
Last week was a sad one in the history of the parish
of West Stoke. The death of 'Lady Victoria,' as
she was known colloquially in the district, was the
one topic of conversation among all classes, and
rich and poor alike felt that a friend had indeed been
lost to them—one, who by her geniality to all and
her open-hearted kindness to the poor, had won for
herself a place in their affections which it will be
difficult for anyone else to fill.   It would have given
much satisfaction to the parishioners had the
honoured dust of their patroness been allowed to
rest in the pretty churchyard, close to her late residence ; but her expressed wish to be buried with her
kinsfolk in the family vault in Wiltshire could not,
of course, be disregarded.   Before the remains were
removed from the parish, however, a service was
held in the Parish Church, conducted by the Rev.
F. W. Shaw, rector and rural dean, and his son, the
Rev. W. A. Shaw, vicar of Hazelbeach, Northants.
Eight workmen on the estate bore the coffin from

the mansion to the Church, which was quite filled
by mourners of all degrees, the air being heavy
with the perfume of many choice flowers, among
them being a wreath from the Right Hon. Walter
Long, M.P., Minister of Agriculture, one of the
deceased lady's nearest relatives, who was prevented
from personal attendance by a meeting of the Cabinet.
The vicar read the opening sentences of the burial
office and the lesson, the Psalm being read by his
son, while the hymns ' Rock of Ages' and ' The
Saints of God' were sung. *Nunc Dimittis*—' Lord,
now let Thy servant depart in peace,' was sung at
the conclusion of the service, and the bearers then
resumed their burden and placed the coffin in the
hearse. The remains of the deceased were enclosed
in a leaden shell and outer coffin of polished oak,
with silver mounting, the inscription on the breast-
plate being :—

THE LADY VICTORIA CATHERINE MARY POLE
TYLNEY LONG WELLESLEY,

Born 29th May, 1818; Died 29th March, 1897.

" As far as Chichester railway station the hearse
headed a procession of sixteen carriages, among
those who rode in them being Captain J. S. L. Long,
the Rev. F. W. Shaw and Mr. E. H. Whitehead,
solicitor, (the executors under Lady Victoria's will),

Mr. A. Fitzclarence Paget, Captain E. L. W. Haskett Smith, Lady and Miss Turing and Mr. Turing, Lady Anson, Miss Anson, Miss Dorothy Long, Colonel and Mrs. Garnham, Mr. R. Christy, Mrs. Kennard, the Rev. F. H. Vivian, Mr. N. F. Shaw, the Rev. W. A. Shaw, the Rev. A. P. Cornwall, Dr. Leonard Buckell and Mrs. Buckell, and Dr. E. H. Buckell, the household servants, etc.

" The same day the body was conveyed, by train, to London, and rested, for the night, at her ladyship's town house, 59, Portland Place. The mourners were : The Right Hon. Walter Long, M.P., Captain J. S. L. Long, Mr. Edward Hugh Whitehead, and the Rev. F. W. Shaw (executors), the Rev. A. Long, Sir Albert Victor Seymour, Mr. A. Fitzclarence Paget, the Rev. Gore Skipwith, the Rev. H. Boothby Barry, Miss Octavia Barry, (her eldest god-daughter), the Rev. St. John Methuen, the Rev. J. B. Fletcher, vicar of All Souls', Mr. Charles Penruddocke (Eastbourne), Mr. E. T. Hohler, Mr. Charles Hill Trevor and her ladyship's butler, Mr. Alfred Lee, and her maid, Miss Mary Horne. The sad cortège wended along the pleasant road from Chippenham to Draycot. The fitful April sun shone, at intervals, upon the hearse covered with pure white wreaths and floral tributes. Arrived at Draycot, the mourners alighted near the Church, and directly in front of Lady Victoria's ancestral home, 'The House' as the villagers used

DRAYCOT CERNE CHURCH.

to term it. The Church path was lined with the villagers, and the Church was full. The coffin, which looked like a mass of the most beautiful white flowers, was solemnly taken out, as the gentlemen mourners stood with uncovered heads. The sun lit up the grey, time-honoured walls of Draycot Manor House. Walking across the lawn were to be seen the three clergy in their robes, the Rector of Draycot, the Rev. F. W. Shaw, Rector of West Stoke, and the Rev. A. Long. The sad procession then moved on. The beautiful funeral service was impressively read. The hymns sung were 'Brief life is here our portion,' 'Rock of ages, cleft for me,' and 'The Saints of God, their conflict past.' A memorial service book, with Lady Victoria's name in it, had been given to each of the mourners as they entered the carriages at Chippenham. The hymns were sung feelingly and well. The plank laid down showed the entrance to the family vault, opened for the interment. The coffin, divested of its lovely wreaths, was reverently borne down the incline. As the words 'Earth to earth, dust to dust,' were uttered the old clerk, who well remembers the Tylney Longs, stood with bowed head and solemnly cast the mould into the vault. The sadly impressive ceremony ended, the mourners went down, in turn, to view the coffin in its resting place. Last, though not least in affection and respect, went down two of the faithful servants who had so carefully watched over her last years and her closing hours.

"There was one niche left in the vault, in which the coffin was placed, by the side of Lady Victoria's youngest aunt, Miss Emma Tylney Long, and opposite the coffin of her brother, the last Earl of Mornington, and also the last of the Tylney Longs, who owned the estates. Never were the words ' in sure and certain hope of the resurrection ' uttered with such hopeful faith as at the close of this sweet and holy life. The last time Lady Victoria visited Draycot was upon the occasion of the funeral of her brother. She never came to the place again until she was carried to it. So with the interment of the last representative of the younger branch of the Longs, of Wiltshire, the family vault of the Tylney Longs, of Draycot Cerne, was closed for ever.

"Luncheon was served for the mourners at the inn at Chippenham. The few words spoken by them showed how deeply the Lady Victoria had been loved and respected, and how much her loss was regretted."

When those whom we have loved and admired have left this earth, words which might sound like flattery if addressed to the living, become but sober truths when spoken of the dead. Indeed, no praise could be too high for the life which Lady Victoria led. Miss Hasker, the friend who had known and loved her since her residence at Albourne, in one of her letters of regret at her loss, wrote this pleasing testimony to her memory :—

" My acquaintance with Lady Victoria, which ripened into friendship, has extended over more than half my life. Our meetings were often far between, but she was ever the same, sincerely affectionate. The long chapter has closed, and I deeply regret that it is so. It is perhaps some little consolation to reflect that she passed painlessly and almost unconsciously away from this world to that better life, for which she was undoubtedly prepared. I cannot imagine anyone in this world of sin more free from it than was our dear friend. She was indeed of a kind and noble disposition."

The vicar of her Church of All Souls appropriately wrote of her as " a rare saint," and added, " For she was indeed the saintliest woman I ever knew."

Her own rector at West Stoke deeply deplored her loss, for he had enjoyed her friendship for so many years, and she had co-operated with him in so many good works. It has been a saying that " no man is a hero to his *valet du chambre*," there-fore it speaks the more for the beauty of Lady Victoria's character that she was so beloved and admired by her servants. Indeed, they could hardly bear the look of West Stoke without her. The numerous societies and charities which she had supported in her lifetime were munificently remembered in her will, for after disposing of her property according to the intentions which, (as regarded the principal legatees), she had for many years faithfully adhered to, there were found in

Lady Victoria Long Wellesley's Will

The following bequests to Charitable Institutions:—

Lady Victoria Wellesley bequeaths for the cottages at West Stoke, £100; to the Incumbent of Marylebone Parish Church for the poor in his district, £100; the Chichester Infirmary, £100; the Brighton Eye Infirmary, £200; the Sussex County Hospital at Brighton, £300; Mrs. Vicars' Home for Penitent Girls at Brighton, £100; the National Orthopædic Hospital for the Deformed, £100; the Royal Society for the Prevention of Cruelty to Animals, £100; the Scripture Truth Society, Eastbourne, £100; Dr. Barnardo's Home, £500; the Hospital and Home for Incurable Children, Maida Vale, £500; the Close Memorial Schools of Cheltenham, £300; the Church of England Central Society for Promoting Homes for Waifs and Strays, £500; the South Eastern College, Ramsgate, £500; the Union of Clerical and Lay Associations, £500; the Church of England

Scripture Readers' Association, Haymarket, £500;
Princess Louise's Home at Wanstead, £500; the
Idiot Asylum at Earlswood, £500; the Royal Asylum
of St. Anne's Society, Redhill, £500; the National
Benevolent Institution, Southampton Row, £500;
the United Kingdom Beneficent Association, Arundel
Street, £500; the Governesses' Benevolent Institution, Harley Street, £500; the Aged Governesses'
Asylum, Haverstock Hill, £500; the Convalescent
Hospital at Seaford, £500; St. George's Hospital,
£500; the Asylum for the Support and Education
of Deaf and Dumb Children, Old Kent Road, £500;
the Association for Promoting the General Welfare
of the Blind, £500; the Home for Little Boys at
Farningham and Swanley, £500; the Cripples' Home
and Industrial School for Girls, Marylebone Road,
£500; Hanwell Lunatic Asylum, £500; the Infant
Orphan Asylum at Wanstead, £500; the Royal Free
Hospital, Gray's Inn Road, £500; the Royal Hospital for Incurables, Hampstead Heath, £500; the
Establishment for Invalid Ladies, Harley Street,
£500; the Hospital for Sick Children, Great Ormond
Street, £500; the Cancer Hospital, Fulham Road,
£500; the Samaritan Free Hospital for Women and
Children, £500; the National Hospital for the
Paralysed and Epileptic, £800; the National
Society for the Prevention of Cruelty to Children,
£1,000. There are also bequests of £500 to the

Army Scripture Readers' and Soldiers' Friends Society; £500 to the National Protestant Churchman's Alliance, Charing Cross; £1,000 to the Reformatory and Refuge Union, Charing Cross; £1,000 to the Church of England Temperance Society; £1,000 to the Church of England Book Society, Adam Street, Adelphi; £1,000 to the Chichester Diocesan Association; £1,000 to the London Society for Promoting Christianity among the Jews; £1,000 to the Missions to Seamen; £1,000 to the Colonial and Continental Church Society; £1,000 to the London City Mission Society; £1,000 to the Church Pastoral Aid Society; £1,000 to Mrs. Meredith's Institution, Clapham Road; £2,000 to the Church Missionary Society; and £2,000 to the Corporation of the Sons of the Clergy. Lady Victoria bequeaths £1,000 for the benefit of the district of All Souls, Eastbourne, and £6,500 to the Church of Ireland Sustentation Fund.

These bequests amounted to about one-tenth of the property she left. " It was a truly Catholic will," as one of the editors to the papers observed. There were numerous notices of her in the various newspapers and reports. Amongst them the Report of the " United Kingdom Beneficent Association " for 1897 mentioned her as one of its warmest supporters. In the Report of the " Princess Alice

Memorial Hospital, Eastbourne," this notice appeared: "The death roll for the year includes the Lady V. Long Wellesley, a vice-patron, and one whose good works in Eastbourne will prove a lasting memorial."

CHAPTER XV.

Footprints on the Sands of Time.

ABOUT six months after Lady Victoria Wellesley's death, Mr. Fletcher took active measures to raise a fitting memorial to her in the Church of All Souls, Eastbourne, which she had built, and in which she had ever taken so deep an interest. The idea was warmly taken up. As the window, which Lady Victoria had herself placed in the centre of the apse, represented our Saviour as the Good Shepherd, those scenes in His life which carried out this idea were chosen. Her executors and friends placed two windows on either side of the centre light. The subjects are : "Christ talking with the woman of Samaria," "Christ pardoning the penitent woman," "Christ led forth to crucifixion," "Christ appearing to the eleven."

On the extreme right, is one window erected by her only godson, Captain Haskett Smith, the subject of which is—"The Commission to S. Peter, 'Feed My sheep.'" Corresponding with this is the

window on the right, erected by four of Lady
Victoria's god-daughters. The subject is, "Christ
blessing little children." These windows, which
are very beautifully designed, were completed by the
end of March, 1898. The entire work was carried
out by Messrs. Heaton, Butler and Bayne, with
artistic skill and admirable workmanship. The
dedication service of these memorial windows was
held on March 31st, exactly one year and two days
after the date of Lady Victoria's death. The
specially appointed service was conducted by the
vicar (Rev. J. B. Fletcher), and was of a particularly
impressive character. There was a good congregation, and the service opened with the singing of the
hymn, "Holy, holy, holy, Lord God Almighty."
The anthem, "O, how amiable are Thy dwellings,"
was exceedingly well rendered, and following the
singing of the hymn, "Glorious things of Thee are
spoken," Holy Communion was celebrated. In this
the vicar was assisted by Rev. F. W. Shaw, rector
of West Stoke, and Rev. H. B. Barry, of Bath.

An address was then delivered by Rev. J. B.
Fletcher, which I here insert :—

"PSALM CXII. 6.
"'The righteous shall be had in everlasting remembrance.'

"We are met together to-day to offer unto
Almighty God, and to dedicate to His service and

M

glory, the six windows just placed in the apse, in loving memory of the foundress of this Church.

"It was my privilege to be associated with that honoured lady, from the beginning, in the arrangements for the creation of this new parish and the building of the Church. Into the history of all that time, we need not now enter. Our present purpose is to give God thanks for her beautiful *life* and her noble *work*. Her *life* influenced many other lives for good, and the power of her *work* will go on for generations to come. In respect of both her life and her work many 'will rise up and call her blessed.'

"In choosing the name for the Church, 'All Souls,' her thought had no reference to the day for remembrance of All Souls, Nov. 2nd, now discontinued in the Church of England ; but rather to the comprehensiveness of the name, to mark this House of God as a Church for the whole parish, a Church for everybody—a Church that should embody, as far as an earthly building can do so, the blessed invitation of the Good Shepherd, 'Come unto Me, *all* ye that labour, and I will give you rest.'

"Only those who were privileged to be often with her, could estimate the joy she took in carrying out this great work. Every detail was a matter of sacred interest. Nothing in the way of material could be good enough or beautiful enough. The whole work of love, from beginning to end, was as 'the breaking of the alabaster box of very precious ointment.' And the day of the consecration of the Church was a holy festival in her life for ever afterwards.

"We all know, too, how complete was her personal self-effacement in the work. She put up a brass tablet at the west end of the Church in memory of her two aunts; but the only remembrance of herself consists of the letters of her name 'Victoria' concealed in the ornamental border of the plate; and possibly very few people have ever known that her name is there at all.

"When she was taken to her rest, the idea of some memorial of her at once commended itself to all. And the form which the memorial should take seemed to be decided by what she had already done. She herself caused the verses of the twenty-third Psalm to be enshrined in the panels of the apse, as a memorial of the faith and hope of her aunt; and placed the figure of our Lord as the 'Good Shepherd' in the central window space. It was felt that this, her thought and purpose, should be held sacred in any *new* work; and the windows which we have to-day dedicated carry out the 'Shepherd' idea, in scenes from the life of our Blessed Lord.

"All this can be studied at leisure in the beautiful windows. But I just mention it now, because I myself want to feel, and I would fain *all* should feel, that her spirit is with us still; and that what she so lovingly desired, we too have tried to carry out, namely, to make this Church, and everything connected therewith, every new beauty added, bring a message of the love of Christ as Shepherd and Bishop of souls, to everyone who enters this house and come hither to worship.

"'The righteous shall be had in everlasting remembrance.' So is the will of God; and He Himself hath pronounced it '*everlasting* remembrance'—*because* they are His own, precious in His sight; *because* their beautiful lives and good deeds were inspired from Him, and tell of Him; *because* He would have us enter into the fellowship of all His saints, even of those departed this life, and be mindful of that great cloud of witnesses by which we are compassed about; *because* He would have our lives lifted up above common things, by our entering in spirit into the heavenly Jerusalem, and joining in the glad worship which ever goes up from 'the spirits of the just made perfect.'"

Side by side with the Memorial Brass which Lady Victoria placed in the west end of the Church to the memory of her aunts, a Brass, the same in form and design, has been put with the following inscription and text :—

To the Glory of God,
And in memory of The Lady
VICTORIA LONG WELLESLEY,
Foundress of this Church,
Six Windows in the Apse and the Stained Glass in
The Rose Window
Were erected in 1898.

" The righteous shall be had in everlasting remembrance."

Over the arch at the east end of the Church is this text, " I know that my Redeemer liveth," which seems to remind one of the steadfast and holy faith in which the lady foundress of the Church had lived. Over the arch at the west end is this text from Wisdom iii. 1, " The souls of the righteous are in the hand of God." Of the three noble ladies whose memory the lovely Church of All Souls perpetuates, no truer words could be spoken.

About the same time, the executors of Lady Victoria caused a tablet to be placed over her family vault in Draycot Church to the united memory of herself and her aunts, who in life were so closely connected by the force of circumstances and the ties of affection. A stained glass window has also been recently placed in West Stoke Church, the subject of which is also " The Good Shepherd," with this inscription :—

To the Glory of God,
And in memory of the

RIGHT HONOURABLE LADY VICTORIA CATHERINE
MARY POLE TYLNEY LONG WELLESLEY,

Who for many years resided at West Stoke House, and died
there on the 29th day of March, 1897, in the 79th year
of her age. " Universally respected and beloved
for her kind and charitable disposition."
She was the daughter of
William Pole Tylney Long Wellesley, fourth Earl of
Mornington, by his wife Catherine, daughter of Sir James
Tylney Long, Bart., and, as the last representative of
the Longs of Draycot, she was interred in the
family vault of the Parish Church of Draycot
Cerne, Chippenham, Wilts.

So in four Churches there will be, to all future
generations, memorials of Lady Victoria Long
Wellesley :—

In All Souls', Eastbourne, the Church she built;
in Draycot, the place she lost; in West Stoke, the
place she loved; and the stained glass window,
erected by herself to her brother's memory, at South
Wraxall, the seat of her remote ancestors.

CHAPTER XVI.

A God-daughter's Reminiscences.

SOME notice of Lady Victoria Long Wellesley, in her character as a sponsor, must not be omitted. It was an office which she regarded as of the greatest importance. Of the three god-daughters, so closely linked together in her will, I was the eldest. Therefore my connection with her began with my infancy. She used to quote to me my father's letter, asking her to stand godmother to me, in which he said, he intended "to call his youngest daughter Catherine, out of respect to the memory of one of the most excellent ladies who ever lived,[1] and Octavia from the circumstance of her being the eighth (living) child." This letter was found amongst Lady Victoria's papers when she died. My father was, at that time, rector of Draycot Cerne, and so had been, in many ways, associated with the family of Tylney Long. But in my remembrance, the "Great House," as it was called, was

[1] Lady Catherine Long.

uninhabited save by the caretaker and his wife, with whom my nurse occasionally took tea, leaving me to wander, at will, about the ancient and deserted mansion. Through a childhood more solitary than falls to the lot of most, I thought a good deal of my unseen godmother. Indeed I thought more of her than many children do of those they are in the frequent habit of seeing. I used to form day-dreams of her, trying to picture to myself what she was like.

One evidence of her was her first present. It was "The Shadow of the Cross," bound in violet silk. When I was allowed to look at it, I used to gaze at it with admiration. As soon as I could read, I must have perused it dozens of times. It made (as my father, in writing to the giver, hoped it would) "a deep impression on my infant mind."

Her feelings as to her duties as a sponsor are shown by this extract from a letter written to her by my father, in acknowledging a present she had sent me :—

"I most earnestly wish that everybody had the same notions you have of the responsibility of the office you so kindly undertook in favour of our little girl. It has often given me great pain to witness the carelessness, or rather the total neglect, of a provision so wisely made by our ancestors for the spiritual instruction and, through the grace of God, the ultimate salvation of the infant Christian. Our spiritual welfare is the main object, and, without a proper care of this, all the advantages which are so highly and justly valued, such as high birth, splendid connections, the immediate notice of royalty, etc., etc., are vain and nugatory.

"It therefore gives me, as a sincere friend of the family, the greatest satisfaction to find that a young lady, who is in possession of all these, is bestowing so much thought on the more important concerns of another life. Your kind and welcome present has reached Draycot in our absence. The letter which accompanied it has been forwarded to this place,[1] but the volume is still at Draycot.

"Catherine Octavia is very intelligent, more so than her age, which will be five in July, would lead us to expect, and I anticipate that in a short time she will be aware of your judicious kindness to her.

"I have nothing more to say about Draycot, which has altered as little as possible for many years.

"We conclude that you and the Misses Tylney Long are quite well. We all beg to be most kindly and respectfully remembered.

"Yours most sincerely,

"H. BARRY."

[1] Bath.

I think I must have commenced my correspondence with her, as soon as I could form my
letters. I well remember how regularly her letters
came, and were duly read out to me. They were
full of such kind and tender feelings. They showed
such interest in me. They abounded in good advice,
and yet they breathed such sympathy that they quite
won my childish affections. I remember, on one
occasion, how one of her letters came looking rather
thick. I climbed to the top of a high arm-chair to
hear it read and to receive a tiny book entitled
" The Life of our Lord." In after years I told
Lady Victoria how her letter had been received,
and she said, with one of her bright smiles, " That
would have made a pretty picture, and have been
called ' Hearing godmamma's letter.' " She used
to write in blue ink, and I have never been able
to look at blue ink since, without associating it
with kindness and goodness. She seldom left
many months without some little remembrance.
Sometimes it would be some devotional book, such
as the " Child's Christian Year," sometimes a letter
with a view on it of some place where she was staying.

At last there came a time when her brother, then
Viscount Wellesley, visited Draycot. One day he
called at the rectory. I felt my small self of the
greatest importance in his eyes; for was I not his
sister's god-daughter! In after years I heard from

Lady Victoria's own lips how she had questioned her brother as to what her god-daughter was like, and how a little incident concerning me had been related to her. Soon after that my beloved father died, and we left Draycot. I rode no more about the quiet lanes, with my donkey as my only companion. I played never more in the dear old rectory garden. We moved to Bath, and I felt torn away from all that constituted life to me. The paved streets seemed irksome; the hills around seemed to shut me in like a prison. I turned away from the bright-looking shops. I pined and languished for the free pure air of my Wiltshire home. Thoughts of discontent and repining crowded into my childish mind. In such a mood as this, one day I got hold of pen and paper, and instead of the carefully supervised letter which, at stated times, I was allowed to send to my godmother, I wrote with no constraint and, I fear, with many blots, a letter full of sadness and discontent.

In a few days my godmother replied. She wrote in a tone of gentle disapproval, pointing out to me how wrong my feelings were, that there were many advantages in Bath, and that contentment was a Christian virtue. I remember that her letter had the wholesome effect of making me feel myself a very naughty and discontented child. The years passed on, the kindly letters in blue ink continued, and, at last, I saw her.   It was at the Misses Long's house in Portland Place.   My fairy godmother realized, to the full, my ideal of her.   She was, at that time, slight as well as *petite*.   She was dressed in soft grey silk.   Her pretty light hair hung down in curls, in a fashion which was then gone out, but it suited her. She welcomed me with warmth and affection, play-fully saying, " You are an undutiful daughter, for you have out-grown your godmother."   That day was happy to me beyond all description ; to be actually sitting by her side at luncheon, to talk to her ! to be with her all the afternoon, at one of the fetês at Regent Park, seemed to me actual bliss. After that occasion I spent, at different times, thir-teen visits at her houses, more visits than I have ever paid to any other friend or relative.

Oh ! the happiness of being with her and knowing her so well.   She was, indeed, always like a fairy godmother.   For each day had some unexpected treat, a pleasant excursion, an agreeable party, or a handsome present.   But the happiest times of all were when I could get her all to myself and have long and interesting talks, in the summer on her lawn, or, in winter, with our chairs drawn close to the fire.

The more I was privileged to enter into the inner recesses of her soul, the more I admired the beauty of her character.   She had such a high ideal of what people ought to be. She, in her meek humility, could never see how near to that ideal she was herself. She was so careful of the feelings and comfort of others. I remember how if she heard I was the least unwell, she would hasten herself to my room to see after me. On one occasion I had retired early, suffering from toothache. The door opened, and she came in with two little bottles in her hand, saying in her cheerful tones, " Here am I ! and here are my nostrums." I felt the very sight of her soothing presence was almost enough to charm away my pain. In little things she was always so thoughtful for the convenience of others. One night she was unwell and I persuaded her to go to bed. " I cannot undress," she replied, " until my maid has had her supper." She seemed to bear with her a certain influence for good wherever she went. It was more from the force of example than from anything she said. She was truly a bright example of what a happy Christian ought to be. She was faithful and attached to all old friends. For dear old Mr. Dear, her rector at Albourne, she always retained a very sincere affection. His visits to Bolney were a real pleasure to her. She used often to quote his opinions. He was one of those clergymen, of the old school, rarely met with now. He really did what has been told of many old-fashioned people, retired to bed after afternoon tea, when staying in some fashionable house. Possibly he was the originator of the story. There was Mr. Reid, too, who used to have a chapel at Worthing and frequently came to spend a day with her.

There was also Mrs. Lyons, the widow of Admiral Lyons, of whom she was very fond. But to enumerate all her friends would be impossible, for she had such a large heart and took so many into it. Her second god-daughter was the daughter of her cousin, Mrs. Smith. She was named Victoria after her godmother and used also to spend visits with her.

When living at Eastbourne, Lady Victoria contracted a friendship with the Rev. E. J. Hayton, (then curate of Trinity Church, Eastbourne), and Mrs. Hayton. She stood sponsor to their only child, who was also named Victoria, which was prettily shortened into " Oria." Lady Victoria was extremely fond of her third god-daughter. She was taken by her mother on a visit to Bolney when she was a very little thing, and she used to delight Lady Victoria with her pretty ways. On one occasion, when she was playing " hide and seek " with her godmother, her mother told her " not to rumple the curtains." " But I want to hide behind the curtain," exclaimed the little one. This artless speech greatly amused Lady Victoria, who was always so fond of children. " No one loved play like dodmamma," little Oria used to say. I often heard Lady Victoria talk of Oria, and although I only met her once, I used to feel much interest in her. She is now Mrs. Howell, of Armthorpe Rectory, near Doncaster.

Our godmother's character was so kind and impartial that I never felt the less an object of her care, because she had taken other godchildren to her heart.

I could fill volumes with instances of her kindness to me. I was often in delicate health, and her care and kindness at such times are very sweet recollections to me. She used to be so tender and careful of my health, and I used to return home strengthened in mind and body. I remember, on one occasion, arriving at Eastbourne after an illness feeling very weak, and how she at once invited me to lie on the sofa, and with one touch of her skilful hand, placed the pillow in such a comfortable position that I fell asleep at once, to her great satisfaction.

It was sweet to be with her after any great trial, to take comfort from her loving words, and to hear her call me her darling! After great bereavements she, in her kind letters, addressed me as "her dearest child!" When my own mother died she bade me look upon her as a mother, and confide in her as such. On one occasion, when I wrote to her with some degree of diffidence, came back these reassuring words, "I delight in your confidence in me." On one of my visits to her she had a slight illness, and while she feared I was dull, I was all the while enjoying the pleasure of sitting by her bedside. I used to look forward to my visits to her room as a rare privilege. On that occasion, too, I had the pleasure and satisfaction of seeing, for the first time, the beautiful Church she built at Eastbourne.

Beside these visits I had other happy meetings with my godmother in London, or for the afternoon when I stayed near Chichester. Twice she came to our house in Bath. Those were indeed "red letter" days to me. In looking back on my intercourse with her, I most of all appreciate the remembrance that her faithful love never left a fault or a wrong feeling unnoticed. If I sometimes vexed her by my pride and independence of spirit, I feel now the most poignant regret for having ever (as Charles Lamb has expressed it) "given her gentle spirit pain." But I have tried to write faithfully, and I cannot say I never pained her, but I can say that whenever it so happened "she was always right" and her advice was always good. Indeed, on some occasions, it seemed as if she were gifted with a prevision of what was best to do, which after circumstances proved right. It is somewhat sad to me to remember that, in the last years of her life, I did not see her for some time. It became an effort to her to receive guests in her house except for a few days. " I have not had visitors for a long time," she wrote in one of her letters to me. But four times she fixed for me to come to her for a few hours, but untoward circumstances prevented these meetings taking place, to my great disappointment. The fifth time fixed was more fortunate. It was in June, 1896, at her town house, at 59, Portland Place, that I met her again. A most happy day it was to me, but I little thought it was the last time I should ever see her on earth. For though she had become more infirm, and required assistance in moving about, she was as bright and cheerful and as ready to be amused as ever. Her last present to me was the Book of Devotions she had taken so much interest in having reprinted, and in the letter accompanying it, she said it was her favourite Book of Devotions which she always used. In the early spring of 1897, on the 29th of March, I received a kind and thoughtful letter, telling me of my dear godmother's sudden illness. The second post brought another, telling me there was little or no hope of her recovery. At half-past two o'clock a telegram reached me, saying she had passed away. So in one short morning I heard of her illness and her death. It was all so sudden. It seemed like some strange, sad dream until I found myself standing over her coffin in her family vault. Then, indeed, it seemed a reality that she had gone. I cannot dwell on the sadness of the next few weeks, when I felt crushed

N

by her loss and ill besides. It has been one of the greatest blessings of my life to have known and loved her. It has been a great and inestimable privilege to have possessed such a kind and real friend. This memoir is the only important work I have ever undertaken without conferring with her. I have tried to do justice, in my feeble way, to her character and her work.

I will now end this little book as I began it, with saying from the depths of a grateful heart, " For ever blessed will be the memory of my godmother."

THE END.

Printed by Curtis & Beamish, Ltd., Coventry.